PRAISE FOR THE WORKS OF
LYDIE SALVAYRE

"One of France's most virtuosic young novelists."
—*Publishers Weekly*

"There are innocuous books that charm you, gently surprise you at moments you didn't expect, blissfully put you to sleep....But there are others, like Lydie Salvayre's novels, that make you sit up and take notice, that directly confront you, that shake you up from the very first sentence."
—*Le Monde*

"Intense, claustrophobic....This verbose three-hander twists itself into a tornado climax."
—*Guardian*

ONE

MAKE A STATEMENT? AND WHAT AM I TO STATE? IF YOUR Honor will allow, these details are of no importance. If I were you, I wouldn't bother with them. You know how to do your job, you say? I hope so, Your Honor, I hope so.

Since you insist, here is how I do mine. I begin the tour with the downstairs gallery. My first stop is in front of the portrait of Mère Angélique. And in a majestic voice I say:

Look at that face. It's ugly. She has a moustache, and a mean, crooked mouth. The jaw is massive. She could be mistaken for a drag queen. And yet, the face of this woman, once the Abbess of Port-Royal, exerted a charismatic fascination on the minds of her time. Why? I ask. Because this face was touched by divine grace.

The visitors then huddle around the portrait of Mère Angélique and anxiously search the homely countenance for the stigmata of divine grace.

What is meant by this? I ask. That our corporeal form is of little import.

What ought we to conclude? I would have loved being a professor, Your Honor, but fate decided otherwise. What ought we to conclude? I repeat. That it is fruitless to cling to things of the flesh, that most deceitful and perishable of substances.

I segue into the vanity of human attachment. I know a thing or two about human attachment. I can vouch for everything Pascal claims with regard to the vanity of human bonds. Attachment to another being, he writes, is folly, first of all because all beings are but fleeting, and second, because they are incapable of fully satisfying the appetites and desires of another.

I occasionally embellish. Especially with groups of German tourists. Human bonding, I tell them, is as fatal as it is futile. For no one can influence the orbit of another. Each of us plots his path irreversibly, awaiting the day of the final catastrophe (you should see their faces!), and it is mathematically unproductive (I love saying *mathematically*), it is mathematically unproductive to link two tangents.

As for the long-term effects of attachment, I continue, they are positively appalling: the reek of promiscuity, the gradual numbing of the mind, pent-up resentment or outbursts of rage. And in the end, in the end, mutual loathing between all parties who have but one idea in mind: sever the ties or be hanged by them.

Tie up an animal, I tell them; for, not unlike yourself, Your Honor, I have a penchant for argument. Observe the animal. Day after day, you will watch it tug at its rope until chafed raw. Then howl at death. Howl at death, I tell them, hoping that death itself might come to deliver it. Then waste away. And die.

Men are like dogs, I tell them. On uttering these words, Your Honor, I think back to Mama, who was as good as dead before dying, and I see her pale face hovering above all my memories. I see a fly land upon her icy cheek and rub its legs together; I see her pale lips closed forever, and her fathomless eyes behind closed lids. And just then, Your Honor, I see the face of her killer who watches with an expression I am at pains to describe, but which fills me with terror; her killer—that's what I've called him ever since I've been able to talk—her killer, whom my mother, from beyond the grave, still makes me call Papa. Men are like dogs, I tell them, Your Honor. They are bonded together by feelings, and their bonds strangle them. And I glare at them if I detect so much as a hint of a smile.

For attachment is love's worst enemy, I tell them: who-
soever ties love down delivers its death warrant. This is what
I keep telling my wife, Your Honor, a death warrant, theo-
retically and otherwise. If I cannot always come up with the
suitably pithy turn of phrase required for a rational demon-
stration, I do prove an excellent pedagogue when it comes to
empirical argument. Thus, every day, I work at educating my
wife. I prod her. I sting her. I attack her. I vex her. I overwhelm
her with sarcasm and nastiness. My purpose is that she rid
herself of me entirely. And I confess, though this may shock
you, that I enjoy tormenting her this way. You'd like some
examples, Your Honor? Here's one that just came to mind.

When I got home from work one evening, my wife asked
me if I bought the coffee.

The chancellery is handling it, I answer, bursting into
wild laughter.

Why such a strange reply? I'm not even sure myself. The
fact remains that this absurd reply brings joy to my heart and
helps me face the recriminations to come. I find joy in anything that foils my wife's excessive cartesianism, Your Honor.
In fact, as a general rule, I find joy in anything that foils
excessive cartesianism or the crushing logic of things. For
not all that is incomprehensible ceases to exist. That's a line

from Pascal. It's written in bold letters on one of the museum's walls. And I repeat it to myself whenever the need arises.

As expected, my wife bursts into bitter reproach. She highly disapproves of my deficiency (in household matters) and my (pathological) irresponsibility when it comes to heavy lifting, tidying up, cleaning and other domestic divertimenti, which, I admit, I hold in utter contempt.

In response, I insult her.

I'll take this occasion to point out that insults and physical abuse, thought to be pedagogical, prove wholly ineffective when it comes to the perfectibility of the human spirit. Does the same apply to incarceration? I don't mean to encroach on your profession, Your Honor, but we might well ask ourselves that question. Indeed, I believe it to be the case that, where my wife is concerned, my constant harassment, rather than making her more detached and impervious, only annoys her even more. It's quite discouraging.

What also never ceases to amaze me, Your Honor, is that these near-daily arguments are followed regularly by periods of calm, where my wife, acting as if nothing had happened, revives her conjugal projects, ludicrous fantasies, absurd pipe-dreams in the form of Olympic-sized swimming pools, mantel-pieces of pink marble inlaid with cipollin, an antique claw-foot bathtub, midnight strolls along the canals of Venice. And for my part, I feign acquiescence, Your Honor, out of spinelessness and laziness, while knowing perfectly well that there is but one remedy against these dizzy ideas: a good slap in the face.

My wife then grants me her forgiveness. By that I mean she assumes her sorrowful, resigned air, then goes about her household chores, in sorrow and resignation.

I have the worst time, Your Honor, putting up with my wife's forgiveness and her sorrowful, resigned face. If truth be told, they drive me crazy. For they remind me of another sorrowful, resigned face; they remind me of Mama's face in the wedding photograph that, to this day, adorns the buffet in the dining room of my father's house. In the photograph, my father is drunk. He got smashed to celebrate all the happiness to come. My mother raises her eyes to the camera lens with that look of despairing goodness that she has worn ever since she met her husband. And when I see my wife going about her household chores looking like a martyred saint, when I see her washing the dishes with her pain-filled eyes opened wide to hold back the tears, when I see her shuttling back and forth with that look of forgiveness, that whiff of victimhood, I want to hit her, Your Honor. I shouldn't be telling you such things, as they could be used against me, but I want to hit her. Your

Honor, because at times like that, I'm overwhelmed by the feeling that I'm just like my father. Could I have inherited his malice? Could he have insidiously taken over my soul, to live on while destroying me? This is what I've been thinking, Your Honor, and these notions are making me crazy, literally so, for I've sworn never to resemble my father in any way; I've sworn it and I'll swear it again, on the heads of my mother and Blaise Pascal together, never to resemble my father. Never.

Enough with the histrionics, I say to my wife, as she goes about her household chores in sorrow and resignation. Stop it, or you'll be sorry. Now, I'm really getting upset. But my wife objects, because of her love for me. For her love, she asserts, is immeasurable. She proves it a thousand times a day.

You would like this evidence brought forward, Your Honor? To set up the preliminary inquiry?

One evening, I'm sitting at the table, waiting for her to serve the Friday evening fare: steamed whiting and potatoes. She's taking her time. I get impatient. I remove my napkin from its ring. So, will we be eating, or should I come back tomorrow? I ask jokingly.

At that, my wife leans over my shoulder, picks up my napkin and slips it around my neck, a gesture that she will later describe as affectionate. (For my wife, Your Honor, love basically consists of treating the other person like an invalid, which in less explicit terms goes by the name of maternal love.) I tear off my bib and give my wife a good, sharp jab with my elbow. It's not that I fear she is attempting to strangle me (that would take guts, which she lacks), but that, at the time, I fail to grasp what she intended. Even at my age, I still fail to distinguish clearly between a show of affection and an act of aggression. Take kissing, for instance, Your Honor. The perfect muzzle? Or the perfect fusion of love? Another example: copulation. Actually, never mind. Let's skip that one. I'm liable to say something dreadful that will likely be held against me.

My lashing makes her cry and snivel. My wife makes a point, Your Honor, of dramatizing her affliction for me. It's her way of punishing me, of drowning me in remorse. At the first sound of a sniffle, I decide to bolt. I rush to the coat rack and grab my overcoat. I'm so irritated that I can't get one of my arms into the sleeve. I try three times, swearing at the goddamn sleeve. And at the goddamn overcoat. Then at this bloody life of mine, and the whole bloody, god-awful world, goddamn it. I'm speaking to you, Your Honor, as you requested that I do, with complete candor. Swearing calms me down. I leave the house. It's a mild evening. I feel growing within me a sense of absolute indifference. I walk into town. I go into a supermarket. I choose a bunch of asparagus. I take it to the checkout. The checkout girl is black. She takes a look at the asparagus and stops, dumbfounded. She goes over her list of produce several times, looking increasingly anxious. The people behind me in line find the black checkout girl exasperatingly slow, and make known their impatience with loud sighs and rolling of eyes. What is this? she asks me, her big, black eyes staring at me anxiously. I say: asparagus. She asks: vegetables? I reply: vegetables. But why in the world am I telling you these things that have absolutely nothing to do with the matter at hand?

Two

THE HIGH POINT OF MY GUIDED TOUR IS INDISPUTABLY the moment when I stop and stand in front of Pascal's nail-studded belt. I assume a contemplative expression. I demand silence. I allow no mockery, not the slightest snigger. A little respect, I say. You're not watching a porno film.

But most of the time, Your Honor, these warnings prove futile. All visitors, regardless of race or creed, are always fascinated by Pascal's nail-studded belt. Just as they're always fascinated by the accessories of vice and all manner of foreign-made sex gadgets.

You need only look at Pascal's death mask, I tell them, turning toward the death mask, which is just to the right of the belt; you need only look closely at his smile, that shadow of a smile addressed to death itself, in order to understand that this sufferer's smile shines in triumph.

For Pascal dies, but triumphs in death, I say, waxing

lyrical. By means of flagellation, by virtue of penance and fasting, through attrition and contrition, Pascal finally vanquishes the roaring lion within. But to vanquish the roaring lion within, he must do . . . what? I maintain the suspense. He must vanquish the flesh, though the flesh perish in the process. I build to this last sentence with a long silence, and I let it fall on my audience like an ax. He must vanquish the flesh, though the flesh perish in the process. And at the very instant I utter the word *perish,* Your Honor, Mama's dead face hits me with a powerful punch, Mama's dead face staring at me through closed eyelids, her dead face with its pale lips and solemn nose, which appears thinner and more severe than when she was alive, the face that singles me out for blame more forcefully than words ever could.

Do you have a photograph of Mama in my file?

Yes, of course I recognize her. That's my mother at sixteen in army fatigues. One fist clenched on her hip, the other raised in salute to the glory of the CNT. In Fatarella, Your Honor. Her native village. In Catalonia. Early in the war, I would guess. In 1936. Why has the right-hand side of the photo been cut off? Because the raised-fist salute was frowned upon back then, and when Mama got to France, she scissored it out of the photo with a snip.

In a camp at Argèles, Your Honor. A lovely camp, Your Honor, with one outhouse for five hundred people, and beds without mattresses. Perfect for rheumatism!

Very well, Your Honor, no more sarcasm.

Yes, it was in this camp that she meets my father. When you're in love, Your Honor, you don't give a damn about comfort.

Yes, that's where I was conceived, in a furtive copulation, one winter's night. The chance meeting of two bodies among thousands of others. And my sixteen-year-old mother who discovers simultaneously the war that uproots people, French camps where hope suddenly dies, and love that makes your genitals hurt.

I'm what they call a "love child," Your Honor. A love child. I've said it before, and I will never repeat it enough.

Stop beating around the bush, you say? Well put, Your Honor, well put. After all, you've got your bird in hand now, so why bother with the bush?

Let's get serious, you say? But I'm being quite serious, your Honor. I'm the very model of seriousness. And I can assert without tooting my own horn that I perform my job with exemplary diligence.

I came to understand, as it happens, that a stern-looking

face would prevent any surprise questions from visitors, the kind of questions I dread more than anything; on my first day at the Port-Royal museum, I knew nothing about Jansenists, save the meager details gleaned from a ten-franc brochure that I strove to learn by heart.

Oh, very much, Your Honor. I like wearing a uniform very much indeed. It contributes tremendously, in fact, to the overall impression of seriousness I seek to convey. What's more, it conceals my natural unsightliness (I'm an exact replica of my Father) and obviates my persistent problem of choosing a mode of dress that best represents my person. If it were up to me, Your Honor, I would dress like Mahatma Ghandi, wrapped in swathes of loose-fitting cloth that would allow my testicles to dangle freely, and I'd carry a large stick to fend off the dogs that abound along country roads. But I fear such an outfit might be deemed inappropriate in these parts, which I have observed to be extremely conventional. And the last thing I want is to stand out.

Grey, Your Honor. Frankly, I don't understand what color has to do with the matter at hand. No, no Your Honor, I'm not challenging the question, merely commenting on it. Yes, mouse grey, with thin, red braiding around the collar and cuffs. All agree that it's an excellent cut. And that it becomes me.

13

No, Your Honor, unfortunately not. No cap. I've always dreamed of wearing a cap. But alas, our dress code does not provide for one.

I nearly missed out altogether on getting this job, Your Honor. I was having trouble coming up with the two thousand francs needed to purchase the uniform, which, I repeat, is utterly indispensable to the proper performance of this profession; for it confers authority, comeliness and panache upon its wearer, while at the same time highlighting a certain storybook quality that's both ornate and totally unbelievable.

When a group of drunken rugbymen showed up one day—Lord only knows why; I certainly don't recall—and disturbed the smooth running of my guided tour with their snickers, smirks and wisecracks behind my back (an accomplished museum guide has radar ears, and eyes in the back of his head), I summoned all the authority granted me by my uniform, and addressed them sternly: You did not come here, gentlemen, to be entertained. Pascal, I continued, had an abhorrence of entertainment. An abhorrence. Entertainment, gentlemen, serves only to deter us from our insignificance. And our mortality. It is wool pulled over the eyes of death, I told them. A bit of nothingness subtracted from an eternity of nothingness.

The rugbymen looked at each other, aghast.

But in his lust for entertainment, man is an abomination, I pursued. He is loath to acknowledge that he is nothing. Nothing, nada, zero. The rugbymen were petrified. Man is garbage, I cried. Garbage! But does awareness of this put him ahead of the game? No, I said. Man is forever doomed to chase his tail. And with that, I burst into wild laughter.

The rugbymen were terror-stricken, convinced they were dealing with a madman. And rugbymen, despite their size, are generally terror-stricken when it comes to madmen.

Needless to say, the remainder of the tour proceeded in an atmosphere of doom and gloom.

That evening, I related the incident to my colleagues, to the delight of Turpin, who has a particular aversion toward athletes. He declared that if Blaise Pascal represented a powerful antidote against the beer chugged down by rugbymen, then Germans should all be administered a hefty dose, a pronouncement that sent Musto into a fit of laughter. Taken intravenously, for maximum calming effect, added Turpin. Stop! Stop! cried Musto, gasping for air between laughs. You fellows are quite unbelievable, sighed Monsieur Molinier, indulgently.

You'd like me to say something about my boss?

I get together with Monsieur Molinier every evening, Your Honor.

Yes, along with Turpin and Musto, the other two guides. Yes.

At six P.M.

In the locker room.

What for? Excellent question. I have no idea, Your Honor. Well, I do, actually. To hang up our uniforms.

That's right, Your Honor. Until seven-thirty, sometimes later.

Well now, I couldn't really say. To wind down after work, I suppose. To get together. To chat. About nothing in particular. All the little events of the day.

Probably because we're back in our street clothes.

That must be it, Your Honor. Our conversations are more informal that way.

What do we have to say to one another?

How in the world do you expect me to recall such things? Nonsense, mostly. For instance, that Japanese women have ugly legs. Like telephone poles. Or that mulatto women, all too scarce, alas, have particularly outstanding derrières. Get a load of that one! cries Turpin, eyes glued to the derrière in question, momentarily forgetting that it has a cover of black skin. That Spaniards always talk at the top of their lungs. The worst, Your Honor, the Spanish are definitely the worst. It's one thing that they pronounce *Pascual* for *Pascal*. But that they laugh their heads off as soon as I show them the nail-studded belt, well, that is more than I can take.

So you're Spanish, Your Honor?

So am I.

It's a real handicap in life, isn't it?

I beg your pardon, Your Honor. In no way did I mean to offend. Being Spanish is a handicap like any other, after all. But when Spaniards go into hysterics over Pascal's nail-studded belt, it can be most unpleasant for the tour guide, when it's not downright intolerable, if I may say so, because the poor fellow gets turned into a circus performer, and the uniform, no longer serving its assigned role of intimidation, now only highlights the overall comic effect of the situation. And in such conditions, any attempt to restore order ends up further provoking the hecklers. If, for example, the guide proposes *Un poquito de calma por favor,* striving to place all the accents properly, they're off again, laughing like hyenas. And the guided tour is reduced to nothing but a series of increasingly hilarious gags, with the stop in front of Mère Angélique's portrait providing the high point.

The crudeness of Spanish tourists is not only a source of annoyance for the tour guide who means to properly carry out his mission, but also a cause of fatigue; for nothing is more tiring than other people's merriment. That's a point on which we guides all agree. We like only gloomy tourists. They are soothing. And there's a glut of them, thank heavens.

If the Spaniard is the enemy of the tour guide, it seems only right to add, Your Honor, since you want the whole story, that the German is his whipping boy. Your average, run of the mill tour guide can feel nothing but contempt and loathing in the presence of a German visitor, with his utter guiltlessness at his own lack of culture. This utter guiltlessness at their own lack of culture is indeed a characteristic feature of the Germans, and the most unpleasant thing imaginable for a tour guide. A self-respecting tour guide derives pleasure from transmitting knowledge to the ignorant, while making them feel (slightly) ashamed or at least remorseful about not being better informed. The ignorant tourist's shame and remorse justify the tour guide's existence in a way and provide him an infinite source of satisfaction. But with Germans, the shame and remorse at lacking culture simply do not exist. Germans are impervious to shame and remorse. Whatever the circumstance, they are proud of their stupidity and of the ignorance in which they wallow. And as is often the case, their self-satisfied imbecility gives rise to the grossest form of effrontery, disrespect and vulgarity. This is why the German is the tour guide's bête noire. And guides detest them. Deeply.

Nevertheless, if I had to draw up the top-ten list of the museum guide's enemies and adversaries, at the very top would rank that foulest of species, the petty little teachers who shamelessly go on about Pascal as if they hadn't just read up on him the night before, concerned only with strutting before their poor pupils. It would appear to be a rather widespread species in these latitudes, the evil twin of the fatuous German, the mentality of the one being as showy, as revoltingly vulgar, as the costume of the other. Vile, Your Honor, utterly vile.

THREE

COULD YOU KEEP ME HERE IN THE INFIRMARY A DAY OR
two more, Monsieur Jean? I'm not feeling well. The rush of all
these memories has my head spinning. And then my cellmate
isn't particularly accommodating, either. The slightest thing
sets him off. It seems he killed an Arab who had asked him for
a cigarette. When the Arab got no for an answer, he replied
quite simply that he could take his cigarette and shove it up his
ass. As you see, Monsieur Jean, my cellmate is extremely thin-
skinned. I hardly dare breathe in his presence. He spends the
day listening to Fun Radio at full blast. I'm at my wit's end,
but to ask him to turn the radio down so that I can read . . .
well, I simply can't. He'd murder me.

Yes, I read.

Pascal, Monsieur Jean.

Blaise Pascal.

You do too? What a coincidence! That's terrific!

Yes, especially *Les Pensées*.

No, no, on the contrary. Talking does me a lot of good. Even the sessions with the judge, which can get pretty rough, calm me down.

Why Blaise Pascal? Because he changed my life, Monsieur Jean, that's why. He has thoroughly changed my life. Reading him has revived my memory. For years, you see, I had repudiated my past. I'd vowed to eradicate it, to let it sediment beneath layers of recollection until it became like a block of granite, like a tombstone. But reading *Les Pensées* caused this past to stir in my memory, like a child in a woman's womb.

Yes, Monsieur Jean, I was carrying frightful events around with me, and I knew that someday, I would have to face up to them. But I was prevented from doing so by some unyielding force, and each time I would postpone the moment of reckoning when I would have to confront my past, darker and more frightening than the deepest night.

Yes, I do enjoy speaking poetically, Monsieur Jean.

You find that ridiculous?

So do I.

No, Monsieur Jean, it hasn't been very long.

At first, I read a few *Pensées* so that I could quote them during my guided tours. Seems to make a good impression, wows the crowds. People like that sort of thing, I've heard; famous phrases, lifted lines. To dazzle people at dinner parties and take their cash.

After a while, I started wanting to know more. But back then, I'd never read any books of that kind. In fact, the only books I liked were war stories and spy novels. I was forever putting off the decision to delve into *Les Pensées*. Why? Perhaps I was afraid of not understanding, Monsieur Jean, and of not being able to get all the way through.

I fell ill in January; yes, it was a winter's day, as I recall, the heavy sky bearing down on the Beauce countryside. The previous day, the only visitor to the museum had been a long-haired, doe-eyed conscientious-objector type. We'd spent the day playing dominos in the locker room, while Monsieur Molinier, with pursed lips and metaphysical mien, attempted to school us in the arts.

I woke up the next morning, aching all over, with a damp forehead and a stabbing pain in my chest. My wife instantly sprang into action. She rushed to get the rectal thermometer, which she attempted to insert. Love knows no bounds, Monsieur Jean, and nothing forestalls its advance. I fought back valiantly, managing to place the thermometer in my armpit, and counted to one hundred. On the television, there was a writer whose name I've forgotten who declared: the French language should be kept in a jewel box. And taken out only on holidays, I said out loud. My wife thought fever had made me delirious. A hundred and two, she cried! The idea of my being sick seemed to delight her. Finally, a chance for her to feel useful. A few moments later, she took on another of my orifices, wanting me to drink down some lime-blossom tea. I complied, just so she'd leave me alone. I'd be willing to do just about anything, Monsieur Jean, to be left alone.

My wife sat down on the edge of the bed. She gazed at me tenderly and suggested I take two aspirin. I declined. I'm convinced that curing any illness is a question of mind over matter. My wife gently passed her hand over my forehead, producing an unpleasant sensation. My poor little pigeon, she purred. Bad choice. I have a violent distaste for these avian creatures that foul public places. But I abstained from responding. I would have given my most prized possession just to be left alone; a groundless hypothesis, Monsieur Jean, since I possess nothing. I then pretended to be asleep. So that she'd clear out. Experience has taught me, Monsieur Jean, that my face must look awful when I'm pretending to be asleep. No one has yet been able to stand the sight for more than thirty seconds. I closed my eyes. My chin collapsed onto my neck.

My mouth dropped half open, allowing a low rattle to escape. A few shudders passed through my limbs. With that, my wife slipped out on tiptoe.

It was then I started reading Pascal's *Complete Works,* which I had purchased three days before with some money I'd set aside.

I read all day.

My wife came in several times to warn me that too much reading would give me brain fever. This untimely barging-in would tear me away from my reading, and each time, I would have to start my sentence over from the beginning. It was getting tiresome—so much, in fact, that I finally said: I think I hear your mother calling. She slammed the door. A welcome gesture. The cat that had been asleep in a shoebox sprang awake, ready to pounce. Then it just yawned, with impeccable grace.

I read into the evening.

My mind soared.

I forgot time. I forgot my room, and the petty reversals of my petty life.

Thoughts came to me, thoughts far above my station. Acrobatic thoughts. Extremely. Thoughts magnified by the effects of fever. Gigantic.

How, I asked, is one to gain a foothold in the void? How?

I looked out the window. Through the panes, I saw night fall. It seemed vast to me. It was as if I were seeing night for the first time in all its vastness. It filled me with fear. But I didn't avert my eyes; I saw the vast night looking back at me through the windowpanes, watched as it slipped slowly into the room, bearing its full load of hopelessness and awesome power. Then, I felt it surge and rush down into my depths, flood my heart, swallow me up and drown me.

I cried out.

Can you imagine, Monsieur Jean, a moonless night deep in the Beauce countryside, you who know nothing but the city light's sham nighttime. Can you imagine this thing coming toward you, slow like a sea, weighty and cold, like a sea, immense, bearing the burden of all that is unknowable, enveloping you in utter darkness?

I cried out.

My wife came running, her slippers slapping the floor. I put my book down. This is going to drive you crazy, she snapped. Will I be able to withstand such metaphysics? I asked myself upon seeing my wife rush in, slippers slapping.

I marshaled all my strength to get up. I couldn't manage. The mental stress had been too exhausting. I closed my eyes, and the image of Pascal himself appeared to me. Then came the image of Mama, superimposed on that of Pascal, and the two gradually merged into one. It was then that I realized the uncanny resemblance between Mama and Pascal.

I called for my wife. I asked her to bring me a five-hundred-franc note. Now. She opened a cupboard and took out a roll of bills hidden beneath a pile of napkins.

I stared at length at the five-hundred-franc note, to the utter astonishment of my wife, who knows me well as having no interest whatsoever in money matters. How is it that I'd never noticed this resemblance before?

Mama and Pascal have the same austere face, the same dogmatic, solemnly set nose, the same arid lips, ill-suited to kissing, the same fine moustache, the same eyes full of infinite goodness.

Mama wears her hair shoulder-length, a detail attesting to her womanhood. Pascal's hair, styled after the fashion of the period, is the same length.

I speak of Mama in the present tense, Monsieur Jean, even though she's been dead for quite some time. Just as I speak of Pascal in the present. For they are both more alive to me than the living.

Mama can claim the moral equivalent of Pascal's nail-studded belt: Papa. Papa is a kind of self-triggering, rapid-fire, nail-studded belt. I have to admit he's fairly well-endowed when it comes to blunt weaponry: huge hands, reinforced with calluses, that dangle at the ends of his arms. Papa rounded off this fearsome array with a number of accessories, including a leather belt worn tight around his waist, which he would sometimes use to fend off attacks by his children.

Mama never complains about Papa's nastiness. For Mama has loved Papa ever since that day he whispered dirty words in her ear, which she took for words of love.

Mama is always worrying about Papa's health, and she never forgets to give him his Equanil pill. It's because Papa is high-strung, Mama says; she never says he's just plain mean.

Because he loves her, Papa can't keep anything from Mama. He tells her everything that's on his mind. For instance, he calls her a little douche bag whenever the thought occurs to him. Which is to say, often. Because she loves him, Mama never answers back. Instead, she merely calls upon a third party as witness (the ceiling or myself), and murmurs: I'd better just keep my mouth shut.

On occasion, Papa beats up Mama. But Mama sees these beatings only as the outward expression of his exhaustion and hopelessness. Your poor father, she sighs, whenever she speaks of him to me.

Papa is stricken with a serious illness that even Mama's love hasn't managed to cure. Papa has a persecution complex. All my life, I've been surrounded by people suffering from this affliction (I am honored to include among them Blaise Pascal, who was, in a certain sense, persecuted by God, the worst kind of persecution), and I've come to the conclusion that there must be a great number of such cases.

Papa sees the whole world to be his personal enemy. His whole world, to tell the truth, amounts to only Mama, Victoria, his darling daughter, François, my brother-in-law, Monsieur Rufino, our neighbor, and myself. I must concede that, given the facts, Papa is proven right. The world, it seems, is enemy to man, and the son is enemy to the father, since the dawn of time.

When in the grip of one of his morbid fits, he takes it out on Mama in particular. He watches her every move, and if anything should strike him as suspicious, he grabs her by the neck and throttles her with his murderer's hands. Mama neither cries out nor puts up a struggle. She says to him: Come, Papa, let's calm down, shall we? Mama, you see, wouldn't for the world want to clash with Papa. Mama loves Papa; I can't emphasize that enough.

And I am the fruit of that love.

Mama resembles Pascal in yet another respect. Mama is poor—poor by nature—where Pascal strains to achieve poverty. But the outcome, all told, is identical.

By virtue of her poverty, Mama has developed a true talent for thrift. Never throw anything away, that's her motto. Hold on to table scraps as if they were treasures. Mama is a real wizard, says Papa, when it comes to making meals out of table scraps. Cooking with table scraps is Mama's greatest happiness in life. Take some stale bread, she proudly exclaims, add a few eggs, salt and pepper, beat it all together with a fork, pour it into a skillet, and you've got yourself a delicious omelet! Mama, Monsieur Jean, is the uncontested queen of omelets. Mama can make an omelet out of practically anything. She'd make an omelet out of stones if there were nothing else at hand. And her paellas are truly inspired, there's no other word for it. A few chicken bones, a little chorizo, a packet of saffron-flavored rice, and you lick your lips.

Papa shares Mama's thriftiness. Whenever I eat an apple, he gets annoyed if I peel away too much of the flesh.

I don't like apples.

Or anything else that requires peeling.

Mama has a further talent that her poverty has reinforced, in a way: she is unmatched when it comes to the price of everyday consumer items. She'll quote you the cost of a kilowatt-hour, or the comparative prices of different coffee brands. Mama has a real gift for balancing the family budget and managing on three thousand francs a month. If she had had the mathematical training of Pascal, she too might have rediscovered the thirty-two propositions of the first book of Euclid and invented the calculator. Mama is a calculator herself.

Mama and Pascal even think alike. They both claim that poverty allows for more leisure time, since it obviates such worries as those associated with managing property and increasing crop yields, cares and worries that doctors blame for heart disease and personality disorders, when they don't lead directly to the grave. Hence, Mama and Pascal conclude that poverty predisposes one to take a philosophical attitude toward life, since it allows us to distinguish the essential from the superfluous and develops both insight and a knack for calculation (both quite useful when it comes to managing a home).

Like Pascal, Mama never complains about being poor. She asserts, for example, that sleeping in an icy room is good for one's health, just as boiled potatoes are excellent for one's diet. Mama never boasts about this, either. In fact, she would be unpleasantly surprised if she were to read these lines. She would accuse me of trying to selfishly prop her up.

Thus, Mama and Pascal often formulate the same opinions about life (leaving aside Mama's compulsion to punctuate her syntax with *shit* and *hell*), and despite the span of centuries, they share the same vision of the world.

Mama says that life is nothing but wretchedness.

She says that wretchedness is the most fairly distributed thing in the world.

Since we're all going to end up in the same place.

The mighty and the humble alike.

Consult a psychiatrist?

Do I seem deranged to you?

Of course, Monsieur Jean, of course.

Wednesday at three.

Very well, then.

Four

My mother's official death came as no surprise, Doctor, since my mother had been dead for a long time when we finally put her in the ground. So that on the day of her death, of her official death, my sorrow was so old, Doctor, I'd been bearing it for so long, that I hadn't the strength to shed a tear.

I climbed up into the attic, and listened to people coming and going, dutifully weeping away. They spoke in a whisper, as if my mother were sleeping, and pretended not to know that the deceased had been murdered. I could hear them murmuring words of consolation into my sister's ear, all the while furtively eyeing the room's furnishings, and presenting their sincere condolences to the old man, whose mind was on nothing but lunch, and who kept asking when we were going to sit down at the table, what time will the paella be served, it's going to get cold at this rate.

Yes, Doctor, we buried Mama on . . .

No, I'm sorry, Doctor, I can't talk about Mother's burial. Impossible. There are subjects I still can't broach, despite the enormous progress I've made since the day I first started reading Pascal's *Pensées*.

You don't understand what Pascal has to do with all this? Be patient, Doctor, be patient. I can't talk about all of it at the same time.

The more I think about it, Doctor, the earlier in time I set the date of Mama's death. In fact, I've concluded in the end that she died the day she met my father.

In the camp at Argèles, Doctor, where my mother arrives exhausted after a forty-day march, a forty-day march through Catalonia, dodging the bombs of General Franco, who has just won the war, a forty-day march, Doctor, with nothing to eat but turnips stolen from the surrounding fields, a forty-day march to the camp at Argèles, and a heart heavy with remorse at leaving loved ones on the nether banks of the Ebre, my mother arrives at this camp more helpless than a newborn, in a camp where my father singles her out among the throngs for her youthful air, her unfathomable eyes. My father, who supervised the columns of refugees following the orders of

General Lister, will go snuggle up to her after nightfall, whisper dirty things in her ear, which she will mistake for words of love; for my mother is only sixteen, and has just slogged forty days through Catalonia to reach the French border and land in the camp at Argelès with two thousand other Spanish refugees, my sixteen-year-old mother, whose life experience amounts to what she learned from a devout mother and the wimpled nuns at the school of the Imaculada Concepción, where the walls are covered with crucifixes and pictures of bleeding hearts bristling with thorns. And this freezing January day in 1939, this most painful of all days for my mother since she loses all at once her language, her country and all those dear to her, this day will culminate in a scene that could mark either the end of her ordeal or merely its next chapter, though at the time she knows not which. In the camp dormitory, where two thousand bodies are packed together, sleeping right on the sandy ground, a man in the darkness will lift up her skirt, caress her bruised legs, and thrust himself in, calling her *mi niña.*

This man, more beastly than any animal, this is my father, Doctor.

And when, after months of wandering in a country totally alien to her, when, after a grueling quest to track down the man that got her with child one dark night (she recalls only his Andalusian accent, a name starting with *M*, Malvida perhaps, and that he served under the command of the Communist General Lister), when, by the most unbelievable coincidence, on the platform of the train station at Brive, my mother meets up with the man she already considers her spouse, she fails to recognize his face. The darkness of the camp had kept it hidden.

Indeed, doctor, my mother was dead before I was even born; she died the day she met my father in the Argelès camp where I was conceived, and her entire life with him was nothing but one long, endless agony.

Oddly enough, Doctor, the idea that my father killed my mother well before her official death is one that no longer frightens me. It was long ago that I was afraid, Doctor, when I was still a child and couldn't know, didn't want to know, though it sometimes crossed my mind that my father's malevolence could produce harmful effects on our souls and leave indelible scars.

What strikes me most today, Doctor, what really gives me pause, is that I could have been in attendance at my mother's drawn-out death without taking notice. To think that, without being aware of it, I stood by every day and witnessed a daily murder. Are we that blind? I ask myself in my prison cell, when the sleepless night sets in, bearing its load of unanswered questions. Are we such cowards?

Crimes are undoubtedly committed in families every day, Doctor, something you're in a good position to know. Every day, souls are violated, confiscated, usurped, tortured and killed before cowardly or unseeing witnesses. And when I say crime, I mean crime, Doctor. I'm not speaking metaphorically, I'm sure you realize. When I say that my father murdered my mother, I'm saying that on that night, in the camp at Argelès, my father killed my mother's desire to laugh, to sing, to say whatever came into her head; he killed her need to love and to do good, finally reducing her to what she was at the time of her official death. A shattered woman.

I don't recall precisely when or how it became obvious to me that my father had murdered my mother well before she died her official death. But what I do know for sure, Doctor, is that my reading of Pascal is what led me to this unspeakable conjecture. Pascal, Doctor. Blaise Pascal. For the moment, I don't know what steps led me to this conclusion.

But it could be, Doctor, that my father may have killed my mother without meaning to, without realizing. Perhaps my father never became aware of what he was doing. Perhaps it never occurred to my father that he hated my mother. Perhaps he thought this was what living together meant—this give-and-take of suffering: suffer, inflict suffering, suffer—that this is what normal life was about, this hell where we hurt one another, kill one another, without even knowing it.

Since Mama's death, my father has been living alone. He's dirty. He smells like piss. His fingernails are long and black, like the claws of some beast. He who once aroused so much terror in me, gave me such nightmares, is today nothing but a feeble, trembling old man whom you could knock over with a nudge. He's gaunt. He's quit wearing his dentures, since he doesn't give a damn how frightful he looks. It's already possible to imagine now what his face will look like in death.

The only thing human about my father, Doctor, is his maliciousness. But there's no one left for him to take it out on. No one left to insult, no one to threaten or curse. It's an enormous hardship.

So he blames it on the world, on the foulness of the world. He talks to himself. He grumbles inaudibly, combining French and Spanish in his swearing. Or else, he talks back to the television, which he leaves on constantly, tuned to Channel One. He talks to the TV. He heaps abuse on it. And with the TV, he always wins: it doesn't talk back. Mama isn't there anymore to say: Come now, let's calm down, shall we? The doctor told you not to get upset, it's bad for your blood pressure. No one to disturb him.

Since Mama's death, my father has forgotten her first name. He sometimes gets it confused with his sister's, sometimes with his own mother's. Nothing remains to recall this dead woman, apart from the wedding picture he keeps on the buffet, for he does enjoy recalling the time when he lived like everyone else. In the wedding picture, Mama looks just like Pascal. Mama often says: I'm ugly. My father replies with a chuckle: Why do you think I chose you? He never misses a chance to be pleasant.

My father gave the dead woman's clothing to the Little Sisters of the Poor. The poor. It's the only act of generosity I've ever seen him perform. The clothing is all black, for Mama has been in mourning since the death of her brother. But after countless launderings, some of the things have turned grey. The clothes are unattractive and cheap. My mother is unsurpassed, Doctor, when it comes to hunting down cheap clothing.

Before my mother's death, my father goes to the movies with other women. But he lies to my mother, pretending to be going out to a café. One day, to get to the bottom of the matter, my mother takes me to the Étoile Palace, where *Beauty and the Beast* is showing. The movie has already begun. We enter in the dark, and sit in the back where there are still empty seats. My father is sitting two rows in front of us. He's got a woman in his arms, a streaked blonde. A whore, my mother murmurs. He hasn't seen us. He kisses the woman, deep and long, his mouth clinging to hers like some monstrous suckling. My mother weeps, digging her fingernails into my arm.

I'm sitting there clenching my fists until they hurt. But I can't avert my eyes from this man in front of us who is indulging in acts I never knew existed, acts that will soon lead me into a murky world, a fascinating, twilight world where, from this moment on, pleasure will always clash with shame and remorse.

You suggest I come back?

Thirty-minute sessions?

Once a week?

Little pleasures are not to be sneezed at when you're in prison.

Next week it is, then, Doctor. See you Wednesday.

FIVE

YES, DOCTOR. OH, SO SORRY, OF COURSE, YOU'RE THE District Attorney, I don't know what I was thinking, excuse me, but you bear a strange resemblance to Doctor Vilemotte. May I call you Mr. DA?

You want me to spill the beans? Which beans, Mr. DA? What are you talking about?

Molinier? You want me to tell you everything I know about Molinier? So you can prepare your defense? But Molinier has nothing to do with it, nothing at all, I assure you. He's just a poor jerk. A loser. A run-of-the-mill manager, the civil service is full of his type. Molinier is nothing but the straw that broke the camel's back.

You'd like a full description of him?

A haggard face, quite the face of a visionary, despite the way his bifocals magnify his pupils.

A skeletal fellow, whose flesh has melted away, leaving his bones and his soul.

A poetic soul, Mr. DA, an infinitely poetic soul that stirs his entire being, perilously so. No, Mr. DA, I'm not joking at all.

When do our good relations start to break down? It's hard to say, Mr. DA. Perhaps starting around July.

Why? Because in July we get a visit from a political big shot, and the visit is a fiasco. And when a visit is a fiasco for the boss, things turn sour for the underlings. It's a well-known fact. Yes, Mr. DA, I'll explain. Explain, explain, that's all I do around here. But my life remains as inscrutable to me as a logarithm table.

The big shot arrives at the abbey twenty minutes late, twenty minutes during which Monsieur Molinier is champing at the bit and gnawing at what's left of his fingernails.

Picture if you will, Mr. DA, those present on the front steps: at the head, Monsieur Lacour, our director, in a three-piece suit despite the heat wave—but when one is museum director, you see, one treats hot weather like everything else: with contempt. Monsieur Molinier is in the background, constricted in his cheap, tight-fitting suit. And myself, a step or two behind my boss (who honored me with the duty of han dling this illustrious visit as a way of rewarding me for, and

I quote, my seriousness and energy). And all the way in the back, Musto, looking pleased with himself, Rose Rigal, the ticket sales attendant, poured into a devilishly attractive lilac-colored outfit, and Turpin, in a bad mood, who knows why.

The big shot manages to extract himself (rather inelegantly) from his limousine, and moves toward us, practically carried by the members of his entourage. Monsieur Lacour walks forward to greet him, and the two men embrace. Monsieur Molinier, flushed and embarrassed, greets the big shot soon after, then introduces me in these words: A quality guide. As if I were a prize ham.

I then invite the gathering to turn toward the museum grounds, and pointing to the surrounding fields with a sweeping gesture, I begin:

In this peaceful, solitary retreat, deep in the valley before you, there once rose numerous edifices, of which nothing remains today but ruins. To your right, gentlemen, was the cloister, at the center of which was an interior graveyard where the nuns were buried without casket. To your left, a Cistercian church built in the thirteenth century by Robert Luzarches, the master builder of the Amiens cathedral. Further on, a farm with its barns, dovecots, larders and wine cellars. But all these buildings were desecrated and destroyed.

By the Germans? asks the corpulent visitor.

I reply with the greatest equanimity that the deeds to which I have been referring took place over three centuries ago.

The political troglodyte leans over to one of his henchmen and whispers a few words into his ear: Move it along. The henchman, in turn, murmurs to me: We're in a hurry.

I then begin my tour with a stop at Pascal's nail-studded belt. Mr. Big Shot finds Pascal's nail-studded belt very amusing, and, chuckling, turns to the mayor, then to the municipal councilmen, all chuckling along with him.

Monsieur Molinier is enthralled with the big shot and won't let him out of his sight, trying to grab his attention by rattling off a mind-numbing introduction to Jansenist concepts. Jansenism's intrinsic nihilism, he recites with an air of torment and affliction, represents, if you will, a protest against the established order, and against the powers that be. Its deliberately aggressive theology and moral message, if you will, not only ridicules human values, aspirations to greatness and heroism, but it also strips society of any claim to justice, and divests authority of any claim to prestige. In the end, this extremist nihilism calls into question any hope of a better society, any earthly vocation, and any . . .

The big shot, who has better things to think about than

the nihilism of Port-Royal (is he thinking about his upcoming banquet? about some novel sex acts? about clever new ways to win over a jaded electorate? Who knows, Mr. DA?); the big shot, I was saying, cuts off the boss abruptly and, turning now to the press corps, declares his satisfaction with the quality of the cultural infrastructure available in the region, as well as its high level of spirituality. The mayor, the three municipal councilmen and all the guests applaud enthusiastically, while photographers click and flash. Monsieur Molinier, a bit disconcerted, vacillates a few seconds before joining the applause. Gratified, the political big shot, with his soft clergyman fingers, fiddles with the big gold signet ring he wears on his pudgy little pinkie—so fleshy that the ring divides it into two little sausages.

After this interlude, I quickly lead the troop to the Manuscript Room. Monsieur Molinier, for whom this visit is crucial (he's hoping for a promotion), hastens to the big shot's side, and insists on personally showing him the copy of Innocent X's papal bull, *Cum Occasione*. Papal bull, papal bull, repeats the big shot, who had no idea until this moment what a papal bull is.

Monsieur Molinier greets each of these exclamations with a big smile. He's in heaven. His zealous attentiveness has paid off. He has succeeded in acquainting the big shot with something new. Minds as curious as yours have grown all too scarce in our time, whispers Monsieur Molinier to the big shot, glancing in my direction, hoping I haven't heard his fawning remarks. The big shot then stretches out the two far corners of his mouth. This would seem to indicate, I believe, that he is smiling.

Two months ago, I began reading a text from Pascal each time I entered the Manuscript room with my cohort of visitors. Either one or two of the *Pensées,* selected at random. Or an extract from his correspondence. Or even a personal commentary on some aspect of his work. I pondered at length, Mr. DA, over a reading that would most likely interest the big shot in the works of Pascal, if only for a few minutes. A few minutes can change the course of a lifetime, I thought. And it became plain to me that, for a person called to hold an important office, *Three Discourses on the Condition of Men of High Rank* was the obvious choice.

In this sermon addressed most likely to the elder son of the Duke of Luynes, I said, raising my voice, Pascal warns men of power against three failings to which they continually fall prey. Primo: the illusion that their privileges are owed them. Secundo: the overvaluing of material goods, causing them to scorn the qualities of the heart and the soul. Tertio: a belief in the immunity afforded them by their power, which leads to the most abominable forms of corruption and to excesses of all sorts.

What sort of excess? the big shot asks in an arrogant tone of voice.

I immediately hear again the voice of my father saying to me: Are you looking for a good smack?

Monsieur Pascal does not specify, I reply, attempting to control the emotion that has suddenly come over me.

It's always the same thing with you brainy types, exclaims the big shot, sarcastically. They talk, they talk. They're clueless. Talk's easy, he says.

Monsieur Molinier, terribly anxious, cannot help surreptitiously gnawing on the nail of his little finger.

At the end of his discourse, Pascal drives in the nail, I continue, striving to regain my composure. I wish to make you understand your real condition, sir, he says to the Duke of Luynes, for it is the one thing of which people of your rank are the most ignorant.

What, in your view, does it mean to be a person of rank in this world?

It means you are the master of the objects of men's base desires.

Why?

Because men are full of such desires. And what they ask of you, to be sure, are the objects of this greed, and nothing but the objects of this greed.

Therefore, do not delude yourself, advises Pascal. Know that vile greed, and greed alone, attaches them to you. And that you are essentially nothing but the kings of greed. In other words, whores.

I like this passage in particular, Mr. DA. Its astounding modernity fascinates me. To think that way back then, no one could yet imagine that, one day, we would become a nothingness-grabbing greed machine. You'd like me to say that again?

I often relive that scene in my head, Mr. DA: I read the seditious text before a more-or-less paranoid, more-or-less potbellied sovereign, and I watch as his face slowly contorts. I am avenged.

I raise my eyes to my audience to gauge the impact of my little speech. I observe Monsieur Molinier. He looks devastated. But then, that's how he usually looks. I gaze at the somebody and his lackeys. They all look devastated. Could I have committed an error?

With my usual sharp presence of mind, I direct the procession to the Portrait Gallery. Represented are all those who were in any way related to Port-Royal-des-Champs: Madame de Sévigné, Madame de La Fayette, Mademoiselle de Scudéry, the duchess of Longueville, Sister Catherine de Sainte-Suzanne de Champaigne, a supreme hysteric before the Lord, paralyzed, then cured by divine intervention, the sexiest and most appealing of the lot, Philippe de Champaigne, her brother, Jacques Bénigne Bossuet, Jean Racine, the abbey Louis Firmin Tournus (his face ravaged by religious rage), the aforementioned duke of Luynes, Isaac Louis Le Maître de Sacy, La Fontaine . . .

The big shot has probably heard of La Fontaine, for he shows a more lively interest in this personage. Self-important, he cites two fables: The Grasshopper and the Ant, and Puss in Boots. Monsieur Molinier discreetly keeps his eyes lowered.

The visit now complete, a certain amount of jostling ensues. The photographers suggest a group shot, and everyone tries to stand next to the big shot. Rose Rigal the ticket girl propels herself into the first row, fusses her curls with her fingertips, and positions her rather extravagant chest in firing position. Try as he might, Monsieur Molinier manages to reach only the second row, to the left. In the photograph, which appears in the next day's paper, he's frowning and furious, and his enormous eyes, behind bifocals, give him an owl-like appearance.

After the photo session, the big shot and the mayor trade a few hushed words, conspiratorial in their demeanor, then exchange slaps on the back as if they've been friends forever. The big shot then does a little pirouette toward our director and promises improvements to the heating, and a shower area for the personnel, both items that were voted on ages ago.

Turning toward Monsieur Molinier, he says, I'm not about to forget this superb visit, his eyes looking elsewhere. This clichéd compliment makes Monsieur Molinier a happy man.

But his happiness is short-lived.

When he invites the big shot to cocktails in the reception hall, the latter's triple chin wobbles in annoyance. He deeply regrets, a matter of the utmost importance awaits him. (We find out the next day that there is a slaughterhouse to be inaugurated in Versailles.)

Monsieur Molinier falls abruptly back to earth. He's been thinking about this cocktail hour for two months. He took the trouble to personally make the selection of petit fours and to choose the brands of alcohol. He went over it for hours with his wife before falling asleep. As a consequence, he's unable to conceal his disappointment.

Mustering his courage, he renews the invitation.

The big shot reacts with the same brutishness as Papa, when Mama would dare ask him to repeat something he'd said. As if I didn't have better things to do, he exclaims, irritated, and he hurries down the stairs, followed by his entire squad.

Monsieur Molinier then turns to Monsieur Lacour, our director who, in turn, slips away, without bothering to provide an excuse.

Monsieur Molinier has lost all hope.

But very quickly his hopelessness turns to anger. And very quickly his anger is aimed at me. We'll have this out tomorrow, he shouts. And he stomps off with furious little steps.

The esteemed company now gone, we chat together for a few minutes, Musto, Turpin and myself. Musto thinks the big shot is very nice. Very, very. A fine person, Musto insists. As proof, there's the rosette of the Legion of Honor that he wears in his buttonhole. I want to make a pun on the honor of the Legion and the dishonor of the Legionnaires, but by the time I put it together, the moment has passed. Always the same. For Turpin, rosettes are like mushrooms. As soon as he sees one, he feels like pulling it out. As for the rest, he has no opinion. He's waiting to hear what Monsieur Molinier has to say. For Turpin's view systematically differs from that of Monsieur

Molinier. He enjoys being the contrarian. Like Papa. Papa, Mr. DA, never ceases to contradict. He's the champion contradictor. The only person in the family he never contradicts is my sister. Because he loves her. Have I already told you, Mr. DA, that Papa loves my sister?

And it's because he loves her that he forbids her to go out, because he loves her that he keeps such a tight check on her friends and watches her every move with the sour passion of a jealous lover. It's because he loves her that he screams at her when she's so much as five minutes late. You're late, he yells; he goes up to her, and he looks her up and down, sniffing out any hint on her face of suspect happiness. It's because he loves her, sir, that one evening during a village festival, he bursts through the crowd of dancers, and like some lunatic, tears her away from François, his future son-in-law. *Vete a la casa,* he shouts. The dancers freeze. Without a word, my sister leaves the dance floor. My father follows her. Mama and I bring up the rear of the dismal procession.

We arrive back home. We can't talk to each other, much less exchange looks. For our eyes are full of something dreadful to behold.

In fact, we haven't looked one another in the eye for ages.

I go to bed. My sister, with her back turned, undresses so

mechanically that I wonder, for a moment, if she hasn't lost her mind. You've got to get out of here, I insist in a low voice. What are you waiting for? Just leave.

My sister knows that our father's monstrous devotion to her is her prison and her plight. And yet she yields, for she enjoys being the rival of a mother so diminished by sorrow and so easily vanquished. But tonight, things went too far. My sister is suffocating. Her rage and distress are too great for her breast to contain. She bites down on her sheets to stifle the cries rising in her throat. I can't stand it, I can't stand it, she repeats, teeth clenched.

Then just leave, it's the only way out.

I close my eyes then to the impending darkness of the night, and so that I might sleep, I console myself that my father's contempt for me is preferable to his love.

Six

My heart aches, Monsieur Jean, whenever I see a Pullman tourist coach arrive, the ones decorated with palm trees, each frond perfect. Because I have the impression that my mother is going to appear from one of them, that I will see her stepping out, with her hangdog look, in the midst of a noisy, disoriented bunch sticking close together to bolster its morale, and that I'm going to see her press forward with those frightened little steps, clutching her imitation leather handbag to her chest, and that I'm going to see her clinging to her husband's arm, while he tries to wrest himself from this human burden, striding ahead in the hope of shaking her off.

This, Monsieur Jean, is why I treat with such exquisite kindness the tourists traveling in Pullman coaches decorated with palm trees, each frond perfect. This is why I guide them slowly, for most of them are elderly, and their legs unsteady. This is why I try to be gentle in my dealings with them, and lavish them with attention. This is why I shelter them, Monsieur Jean, from the embarrassing and childlike fear they feel when faced with things unknown to them, and I try to wipe from their faces that woeful resignation, akin to that of children who submit without protest to the tedium of school.

For tourists who travel in Pullman coaches do tend to wonder what in the world they've come here for, when they were perfectly fine back home, with their cat Fifi, their little vegetable garden and their TV series at seven, a cheerless drama offering tales of woe so different from their own, woe that provides them a respite from their own, stories about inheritances and houses in the woods, complicated by extremely confusing romantic entanglements. But one has to get out from time to time, see the world before it's too late, take advantage of life, or whatever's left of it. Standing in front of the nail-studded belt, they go silent. For everything they see here intimidates them. The vastness of the rooms and the deep stillness. The luxurious paneling. The beauty of the coffered ceilings with their coats of arms. The inconceivable riches enclosed within. The lavishness of it all leaves them paralyzed.

Then, bit by bit, they loosen up. They ask questions. Timidly at first, then gradually more self-assured. The nail-studded belt, is that for rheumatism or what? And if I deign to smile, they all burst out laughing. Then they forget the splendor's chilling effects. They return to what really interests them. They assess the monetary value of things. The chateau plus the grounds, that must be worth a lot. They find that the faces in the portraits look as good as in real life, or even better; they look like they're going to start talking. They're not at all sorry they've come. It's really been worth the trip. And that Pascal, now there's a strange one. The story about the reed, I didn't know that was him. Or Cleopatra's nose either, I'll be damned! The heart has reasons of which the mind knows nothing, I thought that was a proverb. You never stop learning, that's what's great about life. A nail-studded belt, good Lord, to do what with? To think better? The guy has to be a little nuts; people have the weirdest ideas sometimes, I swear; gives me the creeps just thinking about it. As if there weren't already enough misery in the world; ah well, to each his own. Look at that gorgeous ceiling! It's magnificent; how far does that date back, that magnificent ceiling? It's unbelievable how well pre- served it is. Unbelievable. I'd sure take it as my country home. Not me, I can tell you that right now; no, honestly, I mean it; I prefer my little shack. I mean, just to heat the thing would cost an arm and a leg. You better believe it would take lots of cash to keep up a place like this. It's Pascal's own handwriting, look, it says it's Pascal's own handwriting, he wrote it himself in 1685. 1685, that's which century again? I always get it wrong when I'm figuring out centuries. You add one. What do you mean? You add one, and that makes it the seventeenth. You can tell Pascal was a nervous type. Well, it wasn't exactly all laughs back then. And I guess you think it's nothing but fun now? Anyway, we'll never know; that's all just guesswork. Look, there's a portrait of La Fontaine. You know, he looks just like your aunt from Venerque, the same hairstyle. Well, just look at it; the one time we get out of the house, for once we get the chance to learn stuff, you could take an interest in something besides soccer. It says that it's La Fontaine, you know, the one with the crow and the fox. What the hell do I care about La Fontaine, he's not going to put bread on the table. The guy thinks about nothing but stuffing his face; that's how he is, critical of everything. Now wait a minute: not critical of everything, just critical of all the useless stuff. If there's no use for culture, then we might as well just jump in the river. Would you just lay off a little? Here we are on vacation, and all she wants to do is give me a hard time. You'd think she enjoys busting my . . . Come on, stop it; you're not going start arguing in a place like this. I'd like to know what you think is so magical about this place. Just quiet down a little and listen to what the nice guide has to say.

When it's finished, they call me over to pose with them for a group picture. Such a nice guy. Plus, he's down to earth. On their way out, they insist on tipping me. And if I demur, they insist it's their pleasure.

I can't wait till they're gone.

I can't wait, Mother, until you're gone. I can't wait to see you back in your hotel where you'll rest from your pointless, exhausting day trip. A hotel rather far from downtown, it's true, but with all the basic amenities. At the end of your stay there, the group leader will send the director a letter, which he won't read, signed at the bottom by all thirty of you, to declare that you didn't get dessert. In four days, only once did you get to have yogurt.

SEVEN

I'M GOING TO TRY, DOCTOR. BUT I DON'T LIKE MEMORIES. I find them repulsive. Like reheated leftovers.

No, it's not a pretty picture, I'll grant you that.

From the beginning?

I'm barely out of the womb when my father starts trying to scare me. Which is easy for him. Given the relative size disparity.

I take it out on my mother. I soil my pants. I'm already a weakling.

My mother begs me to potty train. She seems to value this greatly. Disgusting, she tells me. I persist in my wrongdoing. I refuse the potty. I have my pride.

My mother has to keep me in diapers into late childhood. I walk like a penguin. And despite all her precautions, I always stink. Pardon me, Doctor, for these details. This is how I became accustomed to people steering clear of me. They want me to be repulsive, so I am. I'm kept apart. I develop a taste for it. And this, Doctor, is how an innocent child, born to be happy, turns into a loner.

I'm taken to see one of your colleagues, a psychiatrist by the name of Pacquin. He's the first in a long series. This one keeps me on for six years. A record. I'm a choice client. I don't utter a word. Nor does he. We sit facing each other, at rest. I like these silent breaks in a short, yet already boisterous life. When we both feel adequately relaxed, the psychiatrist calls Mama into the office. Mother slips him three bills, which he removes from view with skillful legerdemain.

One day, the psychiatrist asks me to draw him a picture. I don't like to draw, but to be nice to him, I quickly dash off a castle with a drawbridge stretching over a moat, with molten lead being poured into it, and enormous killer tarantulas hanging from the ceiling, and balls of fire flying through the air, and tigers in cages ready to attack, and poisonous snakes from Indonesia lurking in corners, and deadly green rays that switch on as soon as someone moves, and diabolical trapdoors artfully concealed in the floor, and which drop open into the abyss, and a terrifying kind of crested fire-breathing dragon that guards the threshold.

So, what is it that you're afraid of, the psychiatrist asks

me. I remain pensive for a moment. If I tell him, he'll tell Mama, who will then tell Papa, who will beat me for denouncing him. So, I lie. I'm afraid of my teacher, I say, picking her at random. She's mean. At the end of the session, the psychiatrist announces to Mama: this child, Madame, is afraid of his teacher. He cannot allow himself to love any woman but you, so he transforms into terror and hatred the love he unconsciously feels for her.

Once outside this haven of peace, the persecutions commence. Mama wants to know what the psychiatrist and I were talking about. She insists. I refuse to tell her. She's dying to know. Did I say bad things about her? My lips are sealed. We get back home. I'm ordered to stay put. Papa is upset, Mother says, you'd better watch your step. It's because of his job, explains Mother (Papa is a construction worker). With what he has to put up with, if we get him angry on top of it . . .

I try to avoid getting him angry. To withdraw into myself, body and soul.

I take up the habit of reading, taking refuge in the closet that Mama generously refers to as an alcove, and which serves as my bedroom. I share it with my sister. In order to sidestep the privacy issue, our beds are set head to foot. Thus, when certain nights find me with a heavy heart, I turn to my sister's feet and confide to them at length my litany of sorrows. My sister does the same. It gives us a feeling of spaciousness.

I read, as I was saying, I read, and read, and read, and I murder my father in a thousand ingenious ways. The ray gun is my favorite weapon. But there's also the machete, the rattlesnake, the cyanide tablet ground up in his coffee. Sometimes, I push Papa down the attic steps. Accidents can happen in a flash. Or I disembowel him like a rabbit. No, I'm lying, I've never harbored such bloody fantasies. Only on occasion do I imagine stabbing him to death. The serial killer craze has yet to spread worldwide. And I hate the sight of blood.

Still got your nose buried in that junk, rails Papa whenever he sees I've been reading for too long. All you do is read that crap, Papa yells, just waiting for the first chance to work himself into a frenzy. Would it be asking too much of you to help your mother out with the housework, you lazy thing? Are you going to get up off your ass, goddamn it?

He's educating himself, Mama pleads, whose favorite role consists of serving as a buffer, and of taking the smacks intended for me.

You want to make a good-for-nothing out of him? Papa bellows, having finally found an excuse to work himself into a frenzy. A failure, like your brother.

And one day, when I'm so absorbed in a pirate adventure that I'm oblivious to my surroundings, Papa suddenly flies at me, his face contorted, savagely tears the book out of my hands, and obscenely mimics wiping his behind with the crumpled pages.

He laughs.

That same night, I bludgeon him to death with a hammer.

Nothing stops these ramblings of mine, Doctor.

No, Doctor. Apart from my sister, I don't talk to anyone about it. I hate confiding secrets. Most of the time, they smell bad and attract flies.

And I loathe flies.

But ever since I've been in prison, Doctor, I don't quite know what's happening to me; my memories are rushing back, and I'm experiencing an irrepressible desire to talk about them. Every day, new memories resurface, great swaths of life I'd thought long forgotten.

Yes, perhaps my current state of isolation has me rediscovering a past, since I can't live decently in the present, nor can I plan for any conceivable future. But I believe it involves something else. A kind of implacable logic has taken hold of my mind ever since I began reading Blaise Pascal, which is to say, since I began thinking. And this logic has restored the minor events of my life to their proper place, and the major ones as well. Certain events that I thought meaningless have started to blossom and assume a different magnitude. Others, conversely, which I held as essential, have swiftly died away all on their own.

My soul is somehow pulling itself together, Doctor, regrouping. I am much more in harmony with it now. But I am, in a way, a victim of its logic.

Yes, especially when I'm at the prison workshop and I'm putting bars of soap into their packages. Images so overwhelming they make me dizzy, and I have to stop working for a few moments.

No, Doctor, they're not memories, strictly speaking. By memories, people usually mean a past whose power is in decline, whose power is on the wane. The images that come to me, on the other hand, Doctor, exert all the force of waves on the sea.

My parents are sleeping in the living-dining room on a green velvet sofa bed they pull out each night after moving the dinner table out of the way. At night, from where I'm sleeping, I can hear their commotion. I hardly need spell it out for you, Doctor. Most of the time, Mama pushes Papa away. She protests in a hushed voice: The children will hear us. But there are times when she gives in out of exhaustion or fear, I couldn't say which. Then, I hold my breath. I don't move a muscle. I cease to exist. But I pay fervent, pained attention to the slightest rustle of their sheets, the slightest creaking of their bed, and I attempt to imagine in the dark the hideous progression of their movements.

Soon, I hear a muffled groan, the collision of thrashing bodies, a mute violence whose meaning is yet unknown to me. My entire being rushes to my mother, as I picture her distraught face, her bruised members, her bullied, defeated body, dead perhaps, dead. I fear the worst. But something tells me that in this nocturnal combat, the worst is fair game. And that I must allow for it.

Stillness sets in. I clench my fists until they ache.

Or I masturbate. And I have the feeling, at that point, that all three of us are partners in the same crime.

Eight

You want me to talk about my sex life, Your Honor?

Well, nothing bashful about you, is there?

Psychoanalysis has given birth to quite a few disciples.

Excuse me, Your Honor, I didn't mean to criticize.

I feel obliged to inform you that, to my immense regret, I have not yet managed, at age forty-eight, to subdue the lecherous beast. And I confess that I continue to masturbate with distressing regularity, despite the paltry satisfaction I derive.

In the interest of full disclosure, Your Honor, may I point out that I was well trained in this practice at a very young age at Boy Scout camp.

You seem surprised, Your Honor.

I shouldn't say such things?

Your Honor is perhaps unaware that all Boy Scouts of my generation, whether they liked it or not, had to take part in group masturbation sessions in their tents. And that not only did they have to take part in group masturbation sessions whether they liked it or not, but they also had to fight off frequent sexual attacks from their camp counselors, whose needs were colossal, if not to say insatiable, and who also inducted us into Christian love with a plethora of biblical quotes. To the immense delight of our mothers.

You're taking notes, Your Honor? Frankly, I'd rather all these details weren't included in my record. They'd do me harm. I know that for certain.

I do feel, nevertheless, Your Honor, that I have at least partially succeeded in quelling the demons that blighted my youth. It's been quite a while since I've ceased to partake in that practice of attempted suffocation commonly known as *kissing*—I believe I've already told you that. Apart from food and my toothbrush, no foreign object enters my mouth. And I'm even more drastically rigorous when it comes to my other orifices. As for copulation, I indulge only on an exceptional basis, since the preconditions required for this act are so difficult to fulfill.

My sex life with my spouse?

Do you really think it advantageous to me . . .

As it pleases Your Honor. I'm not the kind to make trouble.

I confess that ever since we moved to the country, my

wife's choice of apparel does nothing to boost my feeble inclination toward the carnal. The house being large and drafty, my wife bundles up in multiple layers of trousers and sweaters, all held in place with a purple bathrobe made of a cheap, rough wool, thereby doubling her natural volume. And I believe I detect something indefinably hostile and grudging about her unsightliness that's intended specifically for me. An implicit protest, a silent complaint, or perhaps a challenge to be met whose purpose defies my powers of reason.

How far back? You want to know how long ago we last had sex? Does Your Honor really think that this could be of any interest whatsoever?

The courts revel in that kind of thing, you say?

I can answer with great accuracy, Your Honor. June 25, 1994, the day we moved into the country house. A year and six months ago.

That day, my wife wanted us to make love. Was it her response to being in the great outdoors, an inspiration gleaned from the example of barnyard animals, the bracing, roborative effect (how's that for a word?) on her body of a day in the ambient rusticity? I don't know. Out of consideration, I couldn't refuse this chance to copulate, offered voluntarily, as it were. She asked me to choose among her negligees: the red one with organdy flounces, or the black one with the slit panties. The black one, I answered. Whatever, I thought, so long as I don't see her bare skin.

I don't deny it, Your Honor. I've always hated bare skin. Mine as much as anyone else's. And no one, I believe, can boast of ever having caught me totally in the nude. I always go to bed before my wife, thanks to a tacit agreement that allows me to undress in the dark without the risk of being seen. I avoid looking at myself in the mirror or in the flesh, even when certain circumstances require it. I am not blessed with the belief, as was Pascal, that the body is the temple of the Holy Spirit made of airy matter apt for transubstantiation; rather, I see an ill-made assemblage, dislocated, off kilter, all craggy peaks and steep slopes. An aberration.

My wife and I thus set about copulating. Without the preliminary suction of the labial muscles, I hasten to add. I'm far too old for playing coochy-coo, a ridiculous word if there ever was one, but which says what it means. My wife, suitably outfitted, presented her posterior as I had taught her to do, a position that has the advantage of requiring minimum effort and of shielding from view a face frightfully distorted by thermal flashes of pleasure. In order to concentrate, I stared at her derrière, which, for reasons of convenience, she had placed at my eye level. It looked huge. It scared me. I had to get it over with fast. I went at it. We went at it. But we weren't in sync. I moved limply and off tempo. And I felt as impersonal and mechanical as a lobster. Since lovemaking for my wife consists mainly of grunting in tandem, I modulated my grunts to hers. The definition of lovemaking according to my wife, based on the absolute rule of concomitance, is as good as any other, you might argue. Most assuredly, Your Honor. You wonder if I could give my own definition of lovemaking? I can feel all my nastiness rising back to the surface. Deceit and buffoonery—those are the words that spring to mind.

But let's drop it there. The last thing I want is to incur reproach. Disparaging human love is frowned upon by our citizenry, and I run the risk of definitively alienating the jury's sympathy.

With the maneuver complete, my wife got the notion to interrogate me. Did I love her or didn't I? This was the question that haunted my wife, whose chronic need for reassurance always triumphed over her fear of annoying me. Did I love her or didn't I? I was entirely incapable of replying to such an either/or. I was stretched out on the bed, motionless, with no desire to engage in untimely debate.

But my wife's whiny tone impelled me to react negatively.

As a way of resisting, I mentally dismissed her inept questions and set my mind to pondering far more serious matters. Taking advantage of my prone position, favorable to cogitation, I considered a new way to attach the license plates to my VW. Not with plain wire, as I had previously planned, but with electrical wire, more secure, though a bit tackier.

Next, I decided to ponder various means of guarding against the noxious influence of our next-door neighbor.

The landlady had warned us the day we moved in: Hennequin, our next-door neighbor, was a dangerous individual.

It all started, the landlady told us, with the construction of a neighbor's dovecot. Hennequin had realized, only after the dovecot was completed, that it blocked his view. In actual fact, she told us, Hennequin couldn't care less about his view of the village, which, by the way, he loathes. If he's furious, it's for a matter of principle, and solely for a matter of principle. Around here, people destroy their own lives for matters of principle, something you have to understand. The construction of the dovecot, she added, set off Hannequin's persecution complex, an ailment to which peasants are peculiarly susceptible, you know that yourself. To recover, he should have left for America, forgotten the pigeons and their droppings. But he did exactly the reverse. He stayed where he was so that he might keep watch night and day on the object of his torment, and brood incessantly over this abomination. This turned him mean. It proved disastrous. They say he tried to strangle his wife, that he punctured the tires of a car parked in front of his door, and that he poured sugar into the gas tank of the baker's Peugeot. He's forever monitoring the vicinity of his house in a pathetic state of alarm. Every morning, when he's finished tending to his barnyard animals, he pretends to be gardening. He weeds, he hoes, digs, waters; but, in fact, he's on the lookout, just like the animals under his care. And when he trims his hedges, asserts the landlady, it's not, as you might well imagine, for aesthetic effect, which he doesn't give a damn about, but to snoop around and monitor everything going on behind his hedges. For the hedges are his sole passion in life. If he could, Hennequin would spend his life lying in ambush behind his hedges, trimming and pruning, and keeping his eyes peeled for the slightest enemy movement behind the foliage. Nothing escapes him, she says. Nothing. Be careful, she warns, lowering her voice, it seems he walks about all day armed with a rifle.

The simplest way to earn our next-door neighbor's respect, I thought, would be to start off our negotiating process with some form of preliminary aggression, as is commonly practiced with dogs and certain heads of state. But I'm the apprehensive sort, and I never dare confront the enemy head on. I have, so to speak, a literary soul. Mine is an oblique approach. I excel at meandering. I dodge. I circumvent. I strike from the back. I often digress rather than progress.

So I sifted through my thoughts for a tactic better attuned to my personality than overt aggression, and mentally drew up an inventory of the best existing methods for mollifying a tyrant (methods I ruminated on long and hard from childhood, having had the privilege, as you know, of living in close quarters with a despot in the flesh—I'm referring to my father):

– persuade him of my inoffensiveness, and to put it bluntly, of my stupidity (ask him idiotic questions, for instance, about how to plant parsley);

– heartily encourage all his security-minded tendencies: monitoring of fences, fear of thieves, distrust of strangers, etc.;

– bow with the body, while the soul bristles and stands straight (a tricky exercise requiring the suppleness of a snake);

– opt for outright servility, an unctuous voice: yes yes excuse me thank you very much how nice of you . . .

All options duly considered, I decided to pay my neighbor a visit the very next day, and to extend a friendly peacemaking hand, despite our landlady's order not to enter into any dealings with him.

I'd gotten that far in my thought process, when my wife burst into sobs. Since I hadn't been listening to her last few ramblings, I was unable to offer the soothing words that the circumstances required. I'd heard nothing of her plea but plaintive inflections and a few shrill notes, unpleasant to the ears.

Not at all, not at all, I ventured, a stab in the dark.

These words served only to infuriate her, so that she went and shut herself up in the living room, where she let out heavy sighs, hoping, I presume, that they would pierce the wall and rattle my eardrums. But, seeing that I failed to rush and wipe her tears, she hastily brought her little game to an end. I knew that within a few minutes she'd be on the phone with her best friend. How can I leave my husband, she would ask, without hurting him? Then, the conversation would quickly stray to spring fashions and hemlines, ankle-length this year, a godsend for fat knees, laughter, fussing, oo-la-la, la-di-da, blah-blah-blah.

I waited a few moments at the door, then entered the living room without knocking. I'd caught her red-handed holding the receiver. She immediately stopped talking. I pretended to be looking for a book on the shelves, coolly nonchalant and deliberate. She remained silent. I wondered how long she would hold her tongue. My wife's obstinacy is an astounding thing that truly commands admiration.

The next day, I set into motion the project I'd devised the previous night. I rang at Hennequin's gate. Four huge dogs immediately lunged against the fence, barking, standing on hind legs with their claws on the grillwork. These dogs were mad, no doubt about it. All house pets go mad at some time or another, I thought.

Hennequin appeared. Right off, I was afraid of him. He had a compact head screwed onto an impressively thick neck, and something indefinable in his expression that made me think immediately of Papa. He walked up to the gate. I dared not extend my hand through the slit, for fear that the dogs might bite. The encounter seemed to be getting off to a bad start. I said to him, shouting to make myself heard, that we were going to be neighbors for an indefinite period of time. The word *indefinite* made him wince. I at once understood that the notion of indefiniteness could arouse nothing but scorn and suspicion among a peasant such as this. I hastened to add that I worked as a guide at the abbey of Port-Royal-des-Champs. He was instantly mollified and made it known that he sought nothing but good neighborly relations—humane and harmonious were the words he used. He had greatly suffered from the presence of my predecessors, he confided, theater people who led a bohemian lifestyle and didn't go to bed until long after midnight.

Hennequin invited me in. The dogs, which by now had stopped barking, flocked around me, excitedly sniffing my behind. I was unable to overcome a distinct sensation of discomfort. We went over to the sheep pen, the pack of mad dogs pressed against my hindquarters.

Hennequin's sheep came from New Zealand. They had camel-like heads crowned with black horns in the shape of cornets. Hennequin explained to me that if he was cramming two hundred sheep into such cramped quarters, it was a calculated decision, resulting not just from lack of space. He had, in fact, made the following observation: when sheep are given lots of space, they exhaust themselves leaping, running and attacking each other, all of which are useless and even harmful to the smooth operation of the business. So he crams them together to keep them from fighting. His property is undoubtedly large enough for him to build them an enormous covered pen. But this was ill-advised. Categorically ill-advised.

These animals are living in atrocious conditions, I thought. I should have said I disagreed, expressed my indignation. But

I didn't have the nerve. They have horns like cornets, I heard myself say, with a heavy heart. I was acting like someone desperately trying to ingratiate himself, even though what I most desired was to disengage from all human influence, good or bad. Moreover, I was perfectly aware that Hennequin and I shared absolutely nothing in common. Zero. And that any connection was not only impossible but hazardous. As with Papa, I thought.

He next showed me his cows, which were sloshing around in their own manure. I congratulated him. He appreciated it. Hannequin was proud of his animals. He got a good price for them. Eight thousand francs a head. Charolais cattle. The very best there is. I get top price for them because of their soft hides, he exclaimed, giving a pat to one of his cows in a cloud of purple flies.

I searched for an excuse to curtail the visit, so overwhelming was the stench permeating the barn. But I still had to get the tour of the hen house, where I was subjected to the moronic clucking of some twenty scraggly, hysterical hens.

Won over by displays of courtesy to which he was little accustomed, Hannequin came to disclose his personal calamities to me. His dentures caused him excruciating pain. With a subtle move of the jaw, he slipped them onto his lower lip and opened wide his toothless mouth to expose the inflamed gums. I positioned myself before this blood-red hole that opened into a dark, fetid cavity. He's no doubt desperate, I thought, but with a kind of mute desperation, unable to express itself. No doubt, I thought, his life is vile, like all peasants' lives. And in the long-term, his vile treatment of his animals must necessarily give rise to a similar vileness in his dealings with people. To kill a pig that's looking you in the eye with a knife to its throat, to endure its endless cries and the plaintive bellowing of the ewes, to lead the melancholy and docile cattle to the slaughterhouse, to come back out with the smell of blood and dung clinging to his body, to rise at daybreak, dreams halted in mid-flight, to face the icy dawn, the barren land, to suffer the cold and the loneliness, to renounce all the desires and pleasures of society—all this, I thought, could only pervert someone in the long run, and drive him to despair. I advised him to see a dentist. Dentists are all the same, he protested, nothing but a pack of swindlers.

After parting company, I remained a few moments in the garden. The sky was dreary. The countryside silent, not even remotely benign. Thinking back on my visit with Hennequin, I concluded there is no way here to escape from nothingness. For, you see, I use for my own edification such words as *nothingness, eternity* and *soul,* which have come to enrich my vocabulary since I've been working as guide. I have the feeling that these words elevate me, that they would deepen me somehow, but at the same time, that they're dragging me toward something bleak and oppressive that I can't put my finger on.

What in the world has come over me, to be telling you all this? I've gotten completely off the subject again. Could you refresh my memory, Your Honor, as to the matter at hand?

NINE

Should the reading of Pascal be considered a form of entertainment, Monsieur Jean?

Ten

The interviews with Doctor Vilemotte?

I must say, no flattery intended, that I prefer my interviews with you. I get the feeling that Doctor Vilemotte will do whatever it takes to explain me, to figure me out, and that his detached air is in fact only a front. I find that unpleasant. But I do admit that talking does me a great deal of good.

Do you consent to my staying on an extra day?

The infirmary is the one place in the prison where I feel the most at ease. The light is whiter there, relieved of all darkness. It calms my nerves. And I am feeling so very tired.

You want to know whether dragging crowds of tourists around is a tiresome task?

It is, Monsieur Jean, much more so than some might believe.

There are days when we clock more than thirty kilometers. Turpin's the one who came up with that figure. And yet, are we moving toward some greater goal? I doubt it, Monsieur Jean, I doubt it.

We guides differ very little from factory workers or workaholics, with one exception, and it is a major one: that our labors are pointless. Our labors are pointless, and we're proud of it. And on that score, we feel a kinship with artists, with whom we mix on occasion. But this doesn't mean that we consider ourselves as such. With every passing day, we measure the gulf that separates the genuine artist—by that I mean the artist accredited as artist—from us museum guides. One need only observe Monsieur Molinier exerting every effort for the genuine artists to understand immediately that we are clearly not included in their ranks.

You laugh, Monsieur Jean? You find this interesting? You would like to know more?

With us, Monsieur Molinier assumes the fatherly, serenely inspired tone of a village schoolmaster.

Oh no, Monsieur Jean, no; he never gets upset. He's the opposite of Papa. Light-years apart.

Not in the least, Monsieur Jean. He hasn't the slightest desire to dazzle or humiliate us. He simply wishes to develop our artistic sensibilities (which we woefully lack) and to elevate us to the rarified pinnacles of art (those are his words). I often talk about this, for I believe it's a rare and praiseworthy thing.

But in the presence of a genuine artist, Monsieur Molinier undergoes a complete transformation. He puts on airs. He becomes quite articulate. He puffs up with pride. He wants to impress. Impress with what, exactly? No one knows. He carefully chooses his words when speaking. Lofty style. You understand. But his obsessive fear of committing a blunder—a grammatical one, that is—impels him to ruthlessly monitor every word that passes his lips.

This sustained effort of censorship that Monsieur Molinier exerts upon his every utterance lends him the contrite and forlorn air of someone trying to avoid farting. He looks like he's trying to keep from farting, Turpin whispers to Musto, who suddenly bursts out laughing, attracting the perplexed gaze of the genuine artist. Musto tries to stifle his mounting hilarity, but his attempts to contain it only increase the uncontrollable desire. He then turns toward me to conceal from the boss his convulsed face, now bright red with the effort of repressing his hysterics. An outburst seems imminent. It can only be a matter of seconds now. His face is contorted into a hideous grin. And now I have to turn away from him and fix my eyes upon whatever object in the room they alight upon (with the exception of Mère Angélique's portrait) so as not to fall into a laughing fit myself.

During this time, the situation worsens. Monsieur Molinier's features, unsightly by nature, contract painfully and become truly dreadful. The more elated he gets, the more the fear of blundering shows on his face. Three furrows line his forehead, now pearling with sweat, and two disgusting little gobs of white saliva have formed in the corners of his mouth.

The genuine artist, made uneasy by so much pained eagerness, by so much pitiable zeal, seeks an exit to escape all the spittle. And if by chance he should venture to cut short the ordeal of his orator by some momentary show of resistance, by raising any objections, if he should find himself contesting some biographical point with the sole intention of friendly interchange, that's when Monsieur Molinier suddenly breaks down. His machine jams. He begins to burn. He becomes confused. He gesticulates. He overheats. He flames out. He's dizzy with facts and dates, which he cries out each time as if his fate were in the balance. For fear of coming across as inferior (despite the efforts of a lifetime, childhood feelings last until the end), Monsieur Molinier strains to exhibit all available evidence of his culture. It's as if all the knowledge he's stored up for years and years, ever deprived of an opportunity to display itself to the world, were now rising within him like waves, clamoring wildly in his sunken chest to burst from his tight little mouth and come crashing down upon a stunned, stymied visitor, stricken speechless.

You laugh, Monsieur Jean?

Molinier reminds you of a friend, you say?

I like hearing you laugh. It does me good.

But what was it we were talking about?

About fatigue?

So, as I was saying, Monsieur Jean, what exhausted us more than anything, what exhausted my mother to death, wasn't so much that my father was mean, like countless others, but that he was constantly, relentlessly mean. Constantly and relentlessly, Monsieur Jean.

Now that I've embarked upon this confession, which I hadn't for one moment intended, part of which I'm discovering in the very act of disclosure, I must with your permission follow it through to the end.

My father is a lover of justice. He doesn't like human error. He tracks it down. He punishes it. He sees nothing else. My mother, my sister and myself live in constant terror of making a mistake. One of the most serious errors is to answer him. You don't answer my father, Monsieur Jean. That's the law. But a law whose rigor varies with the weather and his moods.

On occasion, my father inquires: Where have you been hanging out again? If I answer, my father hits me and orders: Repeat what you just said! Let's hear that again! And if I repeat, in compliance with his order, he hits me yet again.

I'm punished for answering. And punished when I don't. I've figured out that, in the end, I'm being punished for existing.

My father is concerned about how he appears to others. Outside the house, he's quite likeable. People compliment him on me, such a polite child, so docile. He's gratified by this praise. He runs his hand through my hair. Every time he touches me, it makes my blood curdle. I'm offered a cookie. I say no, thank you. My father taught me to say no, thank you. He thinks that refusing food is the height of politeness. Above all, never give the impression you're hungry. I'd be lying, actually, if I were to say that we're starving. We're poor, that's true, but we're not wanting for anything. Mama is often glad about this. When you're hardworking, Mama says, you're not likely to go hungry.

My father, my mother, my sister and I pretend to live like everyone else. We concentrate all our energy on pretending to live like everyone else. On Sunday afternoons, we take a walk together along Gambetta Way, and everyone waves to us. We're properly dressed. We don't owe anyone money. Our faces bear no signs of anything shameful. My father is a member of the "Screwball" pétanque club. My mother works as an all-purpose housemaid at the Jouhandeau's. *All* purpose. No one dares say, Monsieur Jean, that this work is a disgrace, but I'll tell you, this work is a disgrace.

We're a proper family that stays out of trouble. And no one suspects the crime we conceal.

My father's nastiness begins as soon as we're home and the front door closes behind us. My mother is the first to feel it. My father, for instance, accuses the neighbor of stealing some wood planks out of the backyard. My mother, who knows the accusation is false, reminds him that the planks are in the attic, she saw them up there, he must have forgotten that he stored them away. My father then turns on her, furious. So you're in league with the neighbor, or what, *me cago en Dios!* You're all ready to take sides with the neighbor against me! Against your own husband! He moves toward her. His hand is already raised. He acts like he's going to beat her. Or he insults her. This is how it starts.

If the food's too salty, if a glass gets broken, at any little trifle, my father blows up. Papa has to let off some steam,

Mama explains. You can see he's on edge. Your father will calm down faster if you keep quiet, Mama says.

So we keep quiet. And our whole bodies are quaking.

But our silence is not always enough to diminish the violence that dwells in my father. The violence that flows in his veins. Sometimes he has terrible, angry outbursts. Then the volume goes up several notches. He can be heard all the way down the street. His massive hands begin to fidget. They search feverishly for something to destroy. Chairs, first of all. Then dishes. Then, finally, Mama and me, backed up against the wall, clutching each other in shared terror, while my sister, petrified, stares at us with alien eyes.

My father takes off his belt. His trousers slip down his legs. With the back of his hand, he wipes his forehead, dripping in sweat. He charges toward us, legs fettered, with the belt brandished like a whip. Mother protects me. He strikes her with a stinging blow. I can feel it in my own flesh. And I scream, Mama, Mama! A poignant spectacle.

Let the little one go to bed, my mother pleads in a toneless voice. I don't budge. I remain clinging to my mother's skirts. I'm gripped by a kind of fascination. *Vete a la cama.* Go to bed, shouts my father. I must comply. I wish I could scratch him, hit him with all my might. But I'm far too weak.

I'm enraged, enraged, at being so weak.

I slip under the covers. My heart beats loudly in my chest. I can't sleep. I wish he were dead, I say to my sister's feet. So do I, she murmurs. For hours, I repeat I wish he were dead, I wish he were dead, I wish he were dead. Until I finally fall into tormented sleep.

Have you experienced hatred, Monsieur Jean? Have you suffered the sickening feeling of falling asleep each night with this all-consuming passion, and waking up each morning with that bitter, poisonous taste in your mouth that no liquor can dispel?

Do you know, Monsieur Jean, that when hatred sets in, it takes hold of your entire being? And infests it. And devours it whole.

Hatred, Monsieur Jean, has the power of flies.

At times, my father gets nostalgic. So he sings some flamenco. Or rather, he brays it. But no matter what he does, I hate him. Everything he does is base and rank.

Hatred, Monsieur Jean, is undiscerning. It enjoys the dull mindlessness of flies.

When my father is relaxed, his nastiness is somehow more cheerful. If, for instance, my sister and I are watching a favorite TV show, my father suddenly changes the station, and laughs at the sight of our dismayed faces. My father loves to laugh at the sight of our dismayed faces.

Behind my father's every move, behind each word of his, I endeavor to detect his base intentions, the hidden evil. And I do find them.

Hatred has a taste for dung, Monsieur Jean. Yet another family resemblance to flies.

I hate my father beyond all measure; no one, Monsieur Jean, can imagine how much I hate him. I've believed for a long time that this hatred will be with me forever. It has hold of me. It drives me. I cling to it. In a way, I nurture it. Dare I admit today, however pathetically, that I relish it?

It's what makes me different from others. It's what sharpens my wit and my senses. It's what makes me a wizened child, a child without a childhood, something I'm foolishly proud of.

My hatred subsides with the passage of time, however. For time wields an immense soporific power over hatred, as it does over all feeling.

And if I've now been able to arrive at the horrifying conjecture that my father slowly murdered my mother, it's because my mind is devoid of all hatred, because it's free to think.

Eleven

Do I owe it to your intervention, Your Honor, that I'm now alone in my own cell? If such is the case, then I thank you for it. I can now breathe easier. Naturally, I do occasionally miss the sound of a human voice, and my thoughts leave me not a moment's rest.

What do I think about?

All sorts of things, nothing in particular. I wrestle with phantoms. I see Mama's face. The long good-bye of her gaze before she closed her eyes forever. I see blurry images of my wife, my sister, mingled with other faces I don't recognize. I see the loathsome face of my father. I see Monsieur Molinier scurrying along the museum corridors, with his peeved, owlish look and the arthritic gait of an old man.

You want to know who Monsieur Molinier is? But I insist that he's not . . .

Tangible details? But what have you got against poor

Monsieur Molinier? I feel like I'm rehashing the same things.

I should display a little more cooperation? Certainly, Your Honor.

Monsieur Molinier has a pious love for the arts. And for artists, even more. Here, in a nutshell, is his portrait.

Monsieur Molinier has never forgotten the time Beckett visited Port-Royal-des-Champs. It was winter, and he wasn't wearing socks, says Monsieur Molinier, enthralled. I frankly don't understand what's so remarkable about that, Your Honor. He didn't utter a word throughout the entire visit, exclaims Monsieur Molinier, gripped by the most fervent admiration. We guides, on the other hand, are puzzled at such enthusiasm. Sometimes, the three of us remain silent after a visit, out of weariness or absentmindedness, but that doesn't mean people come asking us for autographs. His eyes were on fire, exclaims Monsieur Molinier, poetically; and the cows they did graze, adds Turpin in a low voice, which immediately starts Musto giggling. Did Monsieur Molinier show his poems to this Beckett fellow that no one has ever heard of, and that he keeps going on and on about? He does stuff like that, says Turpin. I fear he may well have, Your Honor.

Though we do on occasion make fun of our boss's artistic infatuation, and all the spasms of ecstasy it causes him, we do have to acknowledge, in his defense, that his cultural betterment, starting as it did from nothing, was no mean accomplishment.

For our boss had to visit a considerable number of museums before forgetting that his parents were a couple of illiterates who belched unabashedly during meals, farted likewise, and spoke a fractured, barbaric French.

He had to ingest a considerable number of books before ridding his tongue, patiently and painstakingly, of its local idioms and rural accent. No.

But how far away all that is now!

Presently, Monsieur Molinier is fully au courant.

He has seen the latest exhibit devoted to. Outstanding. He has read the latest book by. He tossed it aside. The names of prominent writers cross his lips several times a month. To be praised or pummeled. Depending on which way the wind is blowing.

For Monsieur Molinier presently has very firm opinions.

He knows, unwaveringly, who is brilliant and who isn't, who is in fashion and who is overrated. He knows which artists are admirable, and which needn't be bothered with. It's no use searching, he exclaims, the best artists are always foreigners. In France, he deplores, there are no writers. Not a single writer left in France, he sighs, with a kind of smugness.

We guides, who love our country, we patriotically protest such claims. What about Jérôme Parquin and Lucile Dencourt! And so many others! So many others, for Christ's sake! Excuse me, Your Honor, but I lose my temper in the face of such rashness.

What's that?

Naturally!

When do we get together?

Every evening, Your Honor. We get together every evening. I thought I had already mentioned that.

Where? In the locker room, where we change. After six. Turpin, Musto, Monsieur Molinier and myself.

It's a moment we all enjoy.

To the contrary, Your Honor, quite to the contrary. Monsieur Molinier displays a kindly indulgence toward us. And even if he doesn't go so far as to laugh at our jokes (especially the lurid ones), he appears attentive to our confabulations, intervening most pleasantly and with consummate skill.

You see, Your Honor, Monsieur Molinier's secret scheme is sublime and requires tact. He's utterly devoted to educating us. He wants to convert us to the one true faith, that of art.

Did you know, he tells us (somewhat condescendingly),

that Blaise Pascal was filthy, and thought it vain to wash a body inevitably bound to vanish? This tidbit plunges Turpin into the depths of bewilderment, since Turpin can't conceive that one could be at the same time filthy and famous.

Did you know that Blaise (he sometimes calls him Blaise, like a cousin) that Blaise, as an adolescent, lived near the Saint-Merri cloister, on Rue Brisemiche? The street name alone, with its suggestion of broken buns, gets Musto giggling, which encourages Monsieur Molinier to continue.

Blaise, he tells us—for Monsieur Molinier is inexhaustible when it comes to Blaise—Blaise could not abide someone savoring a particular dish at his table. He called that being *sensual*. In other words, being *dirty*. Rare meat appalled him. It reminded him of something unspeakably vile. Guess what? mumbled Turpin. Turpin, would you please behave. He wouldn't even let them make him verjuice, Monsieur Molinier continues. What's verjuice? asks Musto, out of deference to Monsieur Molinier, who loves to be asked questions. It's an acidic juice extracted from certain species of grapes, explains our boss in an erudite tone that invariably infuriates Turpin. A plate of root vegetables, some water and a little salad burnet, by way of dessert—such were the indulgences of our philosopher, adds Monsieur Molinier. I'll bet, whispers

Turpin, ever the skeptic, into Musto's ear. I'm not buying it either, exclaims Musto, a dash disapprovingly.

Even though we listen to Monsieur Molinier more out of duty and respect than any real fondness or interest, we are grateful to him for being so instructive and for sharing his insights so generously. Thanks to this instruction, we are able to remain calm whenever some rude visitor bombards us with questions for the sole purpose of putting us on the spot and showing off in front of the tourists. I've often noticed that such visitors tend to be unmarried engineers, suspicious-minded, fond of computers and financial investments, who go so far as to take notes during the guided tour (a terrifying sight, if ever there was one, for any guide), rooting around to find some way to turn the visit into financial gain.

Of the three guides, Turpin is the one who greets Monsieur Molinier's lessons with the greatest skepticism. Right away, he's completely bored. He yawns conspicuously, stares glumly at the ceiling. Can't we switch channels?

The fact is that Turpin wants to remain openly uncultured, and not let his head be crammed full by these lectures that are not, strictly speaking, a part of his job description. That's not what I'm being paid for, asserts Turpin earnestly. I'm nothing but a plain old guide, he likes to repeat. Every time he has the chance to enhance his knowledge, edify and enrich himself, as Molinier says, Turpin protests: I'm nothing but a plain old guide. Turpin, you see, doesn't like to learn from others. He takes it as an affront. Much less teach other people. He hates sermonizing.

A visitor who asks him a question could obviously have only one thing in mind, and that's to taunt him. Turpin isn't happy unless he's dealing with absolute stupidity. As for the speech he recites during his guided tour, it hasn't changed in eight years. Not a word. It's all in the way you charm them, says Turpin. And charm, says Turpin, charm isn't something you can learn.

Turpin doesn't like to put a strain on the brain, as he says. Academic types, he can spot them in a crowd. Instinctively. And he despises them. Right from the start. Nitpickers, says Turpin to Musto, who, without saying so openly, harbors analogous sentiments. Big-mouths, pretentious imbeciles, Turpin adds, who has a taste for heated rhetoric. He happens to know a bit about politics. And he's not about to be impressed by these mediocre bourgeois types. He's not going to let that bunch walk all over him, no sir. Who do they think they are, anyway?

Good times, Your Honor? You ask if we ever had good times together?

Why, of course there were, Your Honor, some very good times, unforgettable times. It was only much later that things soured.

You want specific examples?

Since Easter vacation, it often happens that the two of us, Monsieur Molinier and myself, are left behind after Turpin and Musto have gone for the day. It may be vanity on my part, but I believe that, of the three guides, I'm the boss's most cherished.

How can I tell?

The way his face moves, Your Honor. I've become an expert at interpreting facial cues.

To say that Molinier is transfigured in my presence would, of course, be an overstatement; but his lips, usually pursed like, well, purse strings, become relaxed, and the two furrows across his forehead seem to smooth over (a change that has the same effect on me as would a statue coming to life). Pascal, my boy, wrote this ingenious and, in a word, revolutionary phrase: Unable to render mighty that which is just, we rendered just that which is mighty . . . And there you have it, proclaimed Molinier, sailing off full speed on the sublime seas of literature.

I listen to him.

What he says grows on me.

I develop an intense taste for it.

It makes me forget his lugubrious face and larger-than-life eyes behind thick glasses. I even forget that he's my boss, Your Honor, which really says something. One day, he says in passing, call me Jacques, in lofty lyrical tone. I'm overjoyed. I all but kiss him.

Don't go and conclude that I'm a queer, Your Honor. No, rest assured, I'm that way only when I dream. And in dreams, from what I can tell, those things don't count. But as long as I've been alive, no one, aside from Mama, has ever paid me the slightest attention; so that all the favor granted me by Monsieur Molinier really does go straight to the heart.

Monsieur Molinier will sometimes seek my opinion. A signal favor. I yearn to measure up. But I stutter. I stammer. I state the obvious. Or I issue a non sequitur that I immediately regret.

It's just that I don't yet dare speak my mind openly when it comes to literature, though I'm always doing so under my breath, deep down, I mean. And when I do venture to say something, what I have to say is puny and lame, it falters, and proves powerless at reflecting the magnificent shimmer of my mind. Monsieur Molinier sees in me nothing but an ignoramus, I conclude in distress. So I just stand there, like an oaf, as I did with my father.

All I know how to do is keep silent or nod in approval.

Keep silent or approve, as I am compelled to do every time my father heaps insults on his son-in-law. For my father hates his son-in-law, Your Honor. As you might have guessed. Ever since my sister got married, my father has hated his son-in-law. You'd think he were jealous. My father hates his son-in-law with a furious, relentless, throbbing hate. Like a kind of obsessive ardor, Your Honor. One that intoxicates him at times to the point of delirium.

Ten times a day, my father says to my mother that his son-in-law is a good-for-nothing, a gigolo, a buffoon, a *marica,* that he has pictures of Malraux in his room, a *tío de derecha,* that he wonders if he doesn't happen to be Jewish, that he wonders if his mother isn't a whore who's building a mansion with other people's money, that he'll put his daughter in an early grave, that he exploits her, that he takes all her money to buy trinkets, but he's going to teach this jerk a thing or two, and if he goes too far, he's not sure if he'll be able to restrain himself, that *voy a matarlo, me cago en Dios, voy a matarlo.*

We're required to assent to this reprehensible slander. It's an order. If we waver, if we pretend not to hear, my father flies into a rage, shoves my mother, pushes her up against the wall:

You've got no business defending that good for nothing, *me cago en Dios,* that shiftless little shit, *este cabrón.* He starts shouting, they're all ganging up against me, my own family, *en mi propia familia,* he screams, *en mi propia casa.*

My father shouts even louder ever since my sister left.

Since my sister left, his cruelty has blossomed, in a way. It has become more energetic, more fervent. How far will it go? To what insane extremes?

One month to the day after my sister's wedding, my father buys a .22 caliber rifle. He keeps it under the staircase, next to the brooms. Every evening, he checks to make sure it's still there. On Sundays, he polishes it. For hours.

When he goes into a fit over some piddling detail, my father grabs his .22 caliber rifle and starts pacing around the kitchen, weapon in hand, kicking over chairs that get in his way, spinning around suddenly in our direction if he glimpses us trying to sneak out.

Sometimes, Papa points his rifle at me. (The games Papa plays!) Mama immediately steps in between us and shields me with her large body. Don't move, she whispers, and she begs my father to put down his gun.

The Algerian war is raging all the way into our apartment.

Once, when he's holding Mama and me at gunpoint I

murmur: Mama, call the police. At that, my father, who's heard what I said, moves closer, with a face I'll never forget, and he puts the gun barrel to my temple, and says: Here's what they do to cowards. And he stays there, the gun to my head, for what seems like an eternity.

I really think that I die my first death on that day, Your Honor. And all the deaths that follow will somehow feel gentler.

TWELVE

Monsieur Jean, could you give me some sleeping pills? I hardly sleep at all. Every night, it's the same thing. I fall asleep. I hear a cry. I wake up with a start, sticking to cold, sweat-soaked sheets. I then understand that the cry was mine, for I can still feel the path it ploughed in my chest. I fall back to sleep with great difficulty. I sink into another nightmare. The man with the cruel look in his eyes who is interrogating me suddenly starts coughing. I open my eyes. I'm lying in the alcove where I slept as a child. I recognize its blank walls, its oppressive narrowness, and above the chiseled copper thermometer, the enlarged photograph of my maternal grandparents posing awkwardly next to a cardboard automobile on the Santa Monserrat holyday at Reus. My mother and father are sleeping on the sofa bed in the living room, unaware of my crimes. A nameless anxiety bears down on my whole body.

It's then I note the coughing of my neighbor to the right. I tap a few times on the room divider. Aren't you asleep? No. Neither am I. The sound of that voice is soothing. I can see the day dawning through the window out of my reach, and the night full of questions, full of deaths and horror, slowly receding and relieving my heart. I feel lighter. I doze off. Until once again, a cry rips through the silence, the cry of a prisoner screaming in terror at a murder he has committed, the cry of a prisoner who is wrestling on his bed with that assassin who resembles him and bears his name.

Especially in winter, Monsieur Jean. For winter lends more power to the night. And I'm afraid of the night, Monsieur Jean. Since childhood, I've always been afraid of the night.

You are, too? You're afraid of the dark? It's silly, Monsieur Jean, but that little detail about you is endearing. It makes me like you all the more.

Makes you wonder who the con was who spoke of the splendor of the night.

Clearly not an insomniac.

Do you remember that song by Johnny Halliday called *Hold on to the Night*? How could the human mind have conceived such an awful notion?

Do you think the day will come when American scientists will invent a process for getting rid of the night?

Yes, I read at night, of course.

I read against the night.

To destroy it.

And if I were to keep a diary someday, as you urge me to do, I would write against the night. To destroy it. And I would insult the night. I would spit on it. I would call it *Manifesto against the Night*.

You wonder, Monsieur Jean, whether I grasp the meaning of everything I read? Your remark ought to annoy me, but I'm going to try to answer you as sincerely as possible.

There are, of course, a certain number of things that I don't understand in the *Pensées*, particularly anything written in Latin. When, for example, Pascal writes *et hoc tamen homo est*, I really have to wonder what he's alluding to. But I don't get bogged down in these finer points.

I feel it my duty to inform you, in all modesty, that, on a certain number of topics, I have arrived at the same conclusions as Pascal. With no divine intervention, I might add.

There remains one point, however, and not the most trivial one, where I differ radically from the ideas of Pascal. It's the one where he addresses the notion of idleness. Pascal maintains idleness to be the source of all vice and corruption of the soul, and there, I simply have to say no, no a thousand times, and I forcefully assert that idleness, and its first cousin, indolence, unjustly maligned by Christian Democrats, are the most devoted and faithful servants of the human mind. Every day I attest to the accuracy of this position.

No, Monsieur Jean, to tell the truth, not every day. In the off season, I work only Saturdays and Sundays, and for the rest of the week, I have time to indulge in lengthy meditations on human nature, meditations sustained by *in vivo* observation within the setting of the Café des Platanes, the only café in the village. In a way, I replace the Holy Scriptures in which Pascal immersed himself with extended visits to the café, where the atmosphere is very different from that of the Scriptures, but equally edifying.

You want me to talk about this café?

I recall that one day, there's a man I've never seen, leaning against the counter. He's a landlord of some kind.

He makes known his trials and tribulations to everyone within earshot. His latest tenants have absconded with all the faucets. All the faucets, he mutters repeatedly. As usual, I keep silent. The landlord, irked at my unresponsiveness, raises the tone of his plea a notch and turns toward the café owner.

Tenants can't be depended on anymore, they're non-entities, he cries, non-entities. Dirty, thieving, and bad debtors. You just can't trust tenants anymore, shouts the landlord, heating up. French or not, he shouts. Long strands of grey hair circle clockwise all the way around his skull. When he shouts, the strands lift up imperceptibly, without losing their circular form. And I don't mean to shock you, but the damn Arabs aren't the worst. At least they're clean, he says. You have to grant them that, he says, looking at me spitefully. Has he figured out that I belong to the despicable tenant caste? I get very anxious. Luckily, the door opens. It's Pinaud.

How's it going? asks the café owner.

Damply, replies Pinaud.

The lower the land you live in, the damper it gets, adds the café owner.

Pinaud nods and leans on the counter.

Pinaud is endowed with an enormous protruding gut that dangerously overstretches his shirt. In order to redress his center of gravity ever subjected to the earth's downward attraction, Pinaud always stands with his shoulders thrown back. This self-satisfied appearance, along with his curious habit of waving his arms around, arouses in me a childish feeling of fear that I am not always able to overcome.

Well, we're not going to dwell on my woes, are we? asks the landlord, who is probably intimidated by Pinaud's arrival on the scene.

Pinaud orders his glass of red. I watch him out of the corner of my eye, ready to make a getaway if his snide remarks start coming my way.

On the first glass, Pinaud gives a sobering round-up of the state of the world. It's not going well. With the second glass, the world shrinks down to the size of the village. Which is irreversibly doomed. With the third, Pinaud belches. This is the moment where matters move from national and international abstractions to those most intimately personal.

Nothing better than an ugly woman, declares Pinaud (arm-waving), after the aforementioned preparations. The uglier they come, the readier they are, adds Pinaud, sneering (arm-waving).

The café owner doesn't quite know how to react. (His wife and daughter are both notoriously plain.)

Shy by day, wild in the hay, declares Pinaud with alcohol-soaked fervor (arm-waving), and I'm talking from experience (more arm-waves).

If you want spice, go for brunettes, the café owner chimes in, since the topic interests him.

Pinaud pretends not to hear.

You want me to tell you why I prefer the ugly ones? Pinaud asks the café owner (arm-waves and double arm-waves). It's simple, declares Pinaud. The less of it they get, the more of it they want! And he breaks into raucous laughter (no arm-waves).

Discussions of this sort normally make me exceedingly uneasy. My entire being revolts, and I flee the scene forthwith. But today, I stay, fortified as I am by my reading of Pascal, who enjoins men to look their shared wretchedness in the face if they wish one day to attain any kind of truth.

So, what does the Parisian (that's me) have to say about it? asks Pinaud.

Leave him alone, he's shy, says the café owner, who doesn't care to lose one of his customers.

An anxious silence ensues.

Get laid once, get laid twice! And then what? pursues the café owner.

What is man in the infinite? I say, feeling emboldened all of a sudden.

Not a whole lot, says the landlord.

A pile of shit, says Pinaud, suddenly dejected.

If that, says the café owner.

A dim-witted worm, I say, after a long inner struggle.

You can say that again, says Pinaud, without looking at me.

At that juncture, in walks Perrachon.

How's it going? asks the café owner.

By plane, says Perrachon.

Pinaud acts like he's going to be sick.

Okay, one more for the road, to forget that the Earth is overrun by a gang of assholes, says Pinaud to the café owner (arm-waves).

Yes sir, a guy has to wet his whistle, says the landlord in approval, intended for Pinaud (impassive), in a final attempt to charm.

Ciao, ciao, bambino, I say, conforming to the bantering tone. And I walk out into the open air.

When I get home:

You're late, my wife says.

These words remind me of someone.

You're late, she repeats.

Even when you have nerves of steel, it's exceedingly tiresome to be greeted with this sort of remark.

It's exceedingly tiresome, what's more, to be the object of someone's expectations. Or the sole object of their love. Or their sole victim. Which amounts to the same thing. And yet, here I am, having become, through an unfortunate coincidence, the center, the target, I should say, of my wife's concern. You're all I have in the world, she tells me, ever since we moved to the countryside.

A chilling declaration.

It's just that my wife's life, which wasn't much before, isn't anything at all now.

My wife is bored to death out here in the country. To the point where she wonders whether she might not be better off going back to work at the shirt factory, where she worked before we were married.

My wife, Monsieur Jean, doesn't even have a baby whose excrement she could attend to for entertainment. Or a little daughter she could join forces with against me, as tradition has it. Or a little boy that she could slap around at will because he got chocolate all over the wall, somebody she could take out her vengeance on with no fear of reprisal. Or a poodle. To groom.

No matter how hard she ponders the matter, my wife doesn't know what to do with her time, which she mistakenly calls free. How to fill it? How to kill it?

You see, my wife doesn't like to embroider doilies for the TV set, or gossip with the local peasant women—they smell bad—or sing in the parish choir on Saturday afternoons between the butcher's wife, who sings off key, and the gas station attendant's wife, who lisps. Nor does she care to phone her mother to get her potato casserole recipe—it costs good money—or take walks in the countryside—it reeks of manure and the sky is the color of a corpse—or spend the day at the shopping center dreaming wistfully in front of store windows: what's the use in that?

What to do, then?

Hope. Then lose hope.

Then the other way around.

My wife is always saying, Monsieur Jean, that, what with the dreary life she's living out here, she going to end up completely crazy. And at times, I fear she might be right. She's alone all day long, you see, and madness tends to prey on the lonely.

We often imagine that the countryside is ideal for rest and reflection. But it's just the opposite. You have to plunge headlong into exhausting pursuits such as gardening, wood chopping or exercising, if you want to fend off the silence and loneliness that so relentlessly assail and destroy your brain. And you realize in no time that it's impossible to think in the midst of such hostility.

And what's more, time speeds up out here. You have to figure one minute in the country for every fifteen minutes in

111

the city. The onset of aging is faster than anywhere else, as a consequence. I've checked it out on my wife's body, which is withering away with each passing day. I can read it in the ugliness of her face, which is more irreparable with each passing day. My wife is not being worn out by the daily grind of housework, as she may think. My wife is being worn out by the hideous grind of time.

And in periods of expectancy, time flows even more slowly, with an infinite sadness permeating all things, and every hour that passes is a desert to be crossed. So her mind starts spinning and spewing, a sick brain churning out demented ideas, she suddenly gets the notion that the world has petrified, that she's been abandoned for good, that she's moving through an endless tunnel, or that she's freefalling into the void, it's dreadful, you're the only one I can hold on to, she says to me.

In a way, Monsieur Jean, I'm the only animated object that my wife has at her disposal. Since I still talk. Since I still get a hard-on—rarely, but I still do. And since, at least according to appearances, I'm alive.

You're late, my wife says.

I was thinking, I tell her.

About what? my wife asks.

About earthworms, I say.

About earthworms? cries my wife.

About earthworms, I say.

And why about earthworms? she asks.

Because I resemble them, I say.

She bursts into hysterical laughter.

You resemble them? she says.

I resemble them, I say.

Stop making me laugh so hard, she says.

The grandeur of man lies in his awareness that he is a worm. I'm trying my hand at literary discourse, and I feel a secret sense of pride in it.

And you think this is the kind of notion that will get you ahead in the world? gloats my wife.

You've probably guessed, Monsieur Jean, that my wife and I have reached a high degree of specialization when it comes to arguing, thanks to regular practice and intrinsic personal qualities. I've noticed, moreover, that lately our warm-up periods have been getting shorter and shorter, leaving us more time for our actual quarrels.

Are these arguments preferable to nothing at all? That's the question I often ask myself.

In any case, these arguments can go on for hours, days even, and give me, as does God, a certain idea of the infinite.

In general, they come to an end only after threats have piled upon threats, insults upon insults, tears upon tears, and I pound my fist on the table, or I hit her, goddamn it.

And the more she screams, the more I hit her.

The next day, it starts all over again. The same rebukes spat out, the same cruelties shouted between sobs, the same grievances trotted out a hundred times, low blows, feints, lies, betrayals, denials, red nose and snot running down, mixing with the tears. One has to keep busy.

You're also a miserable earthworm, I tell my wife.

Your nastiness will be your ruin, she says.

Thirteen

Your nastiness will be your ruin, says my wife.

As you may have guessed, Your Honor, the question of nastiness is not without interest for me. Indeed, it is not uncommon for my wife to call me nasty, and for acts that, strictly speaking, do not fall under the category of nastiness. So that you might gauge the unfairness of such an allegation, here are a few examples of what my wife considers as incontrovertible evidence of my nastiness, when I:

– withdraw into myself to get some peace and quiet;

– defend myself against the ceaseless trespassing on the lawn of my spiritual life. Rather nicely put, wouldn't you say, Your Honor?;

– take a dump in peace (hours at a stretch, until my wife, infuriated, screams from behind the door: Are you dead in there, or what?), as well as other activities, solitary by definition and structurally associated with meditation;

– spurn the affection of others when it appears motivated by something unwholesome (love, fear of the cold, etc.);

– lose my illusions, and state as much, clearly and openly (the most unpardonable form of cruelty there is);

– show some diffidence when it comes to a certain number of festive occasions, such as Mother's Day, Father's Day, New Year's Eve, weddings (which Pascal regarded, and rightly so, as a form of murder, letter to Mademoiselle de Roannez, page such and such), cocktail parties of any kind, Bastille Day. In truth, the only thing I can stand are funerals, which are quite peaceful in these parts, entertaining, of course, but quite peaceful, nonetheless, and perfectly propitious, fair weather permitting, to philosophical reflection. Since I haven't a friend to my name, the opportunities for attending one are, alas, exceptionally rare (the last one I attended was Mama's), to my great regret.

If I call attention to this matter of nastiness, Your Honor, it is because it would upset me terribly if you were to hastily conclude, from my wife's allegations and from my criminal act, that I am by nature a malicious person. You'd be mistaken.

I think, Your Honor, to the extent that what I think matters to you, I think it is absolutely vital during this trial that a distinction be made between two broad varieties of malicious people: the person who is evil by nature or by vocation (Papa, Jack the Ripper, Stalin, Hitler, etc.) and the person who is only occasionally malicious (of which I am a sorry example).

The more I look at the portrait of the French President hanging right above your head, Your Honor, the more I believe that these questions deserve a thorough examination.

In the category of the person malicious by vocation, there is the historical case, adored by the throngs, short in stature, his face already sculpted, statue-like, in anticipation of posterity, and who appears, like the moon, at regular intervals . . .

You'd appreciate it if I could be brief, Your Honor?

If I got back to my story?

So, where were we?

Ah yes. Your nastiness will be your ruin, prophesizes my wife.

Ordinarily, Your Honor, when accusations of that sort are brought against me, either I remain silent, or I retaliate, or I stupidly throw a fit. But whatever the case, I experience shame, a vague unease, the feeling of guilt for some unidentifiable misdeed. So, I repent. Then I repent having repented. Then . . . well, you're familiar enough with these pathetic states of mind, aren't you?

That particular day, I remain impassive. Within and without. My dear, I say, with no animosity whatsoever, I don't try to conceal my flaws, as the majority of subjugated people do. For it is doubtless wrong to be full of faults; but it is a still greater wrong to be full of them and to be unwilling to recognize them. (I read that *Pensée* on my walk home, and I committed it to memory.)

Quite satisfied with my little speech, I sink back into my ratine armchair and turn on the television.

My wife comes and sits next to me, all color drained from her face, and (in case I might not have noticed her sickly complexion) starts kneading her stomach with a gentle hand, a warning sign that our argument is liable to escalate further.

Focusing on the brainteaser game show, I try to make a word out of the letters S, Z, K, U, C, O, and P, but all I find is SUCK.

Your feet! snaps my wife, irritably.

For a few moments, I make an effort to control my extremities, which tend naturally to fidget as soon as I'm in front of my TV set.

A remark is in order here. My wife, by way of a psycho-logical mechanism well known among psychiatrists, has taken an intense dislike to the habit I have of jiggling my feet when I'm sitting in front of my TV. And by focusing her resentment on this tiny part of my person, on such poor, inoffensive things as my feet, she is able to put up with the rest of me cheerfully.

Your feet, screams my wife, a few moments later, the irrepressible movement of my feet having resumed without my noticing.

I feel I'm about to lose my composure. But, no. Remain calm. Hold back. I'm going to take a dump, I say to myself. When I get back, things will have calmed down.

My greatest wish, which I confess remains yet unfulfilled, is to attain the wisdom of my cat. In the pursuit of this feline ideal, I can pride myself in having achieved a tiny part. I've recently been able to pursue my penchants, though they may change as quickly as a Siamese cat's whiskers, and to switch my outlook and direction in a wink. If today I'm awed by Pascal, it's just as likely that by tomorrow, I'll have forgotten him. Enormous progress, if I compare my current attitude to that of my youth, steeped in unwavering indignation, unwavering admirations and unwavering convictions.

Since then, everything in me wavers, but does so to my own heart's desire.

Back from the toilet, I ask my wife if she's ready. We're invited over for the first (and last) time to Monsieur Molinier's, and it would be vexing to arrive late.

We get into the car. I start the engine and we're off. The turn signal, says my wife. I head toward Versailles. I'm relaxed. I feel as if I'm escaping from the night which is parted in two by the headlights. Slower, mutters my wife, you're too far to the right. I turn on the radio. The anchovy war is in full swing. The Spanish seem to be winning. No casualties yet on the French side. I slow down at an intersection to better read the road signs. The second one, orders my wife. She's starting to annoy me. The second one, she repeats, sounding irate. I go around a bend to the left. Slow down, my wife orders. She's annoying me, annoying me, annoying me! Slow down, she repeats. Shut up, I say then, completely fed up, and I step on the gas with everything I've got. You're going to get us killed, cries my wife, stamping on an imaginary brake pedal. Get this through your thick head, I reply, moving at top speed, I am almost as despicable as Papa, that's a fact, but unlike the majority of men, I don't try to pass it off as better. Most men, I tell her, abhor the truth about themselves. They'd rather be flattered. They gorge themselves on lies, grow fat on them. They choose as friends those who fawn on them most convincingly. This is why I have no friends, I say, bearing down on the gas pedal with wicked delight. And no love, I conclude, in a final burst of nastiness.

Fourteen

My mother occasionally forgets that she's dead, and laughs from behind her sewing machine, and devours my cheeks in passionate kisses. Get a divorce! I tell her. Marry Monsieur Anzar, who gives me an orange every time I pass by his fruit stand. Or let's go away and live in Fatarella, where she was born, near your sister Consuelo (the one with the forearms of a butcher and the strength of a black belt). Get a divorce, then we'll leave together, I tell her.

My mother laughs with a young girl's lilt. The same laugh that sets her face aglow in the photograph where she's posing in a soldier's uniform, fist raised.

But her laughter fades as soon as my father walks through the door.

And my mother resumes her dying.

—✦—

A memory comes to mind, Doctor.

We're sitting around the dinner table. It's eight o'clock in the evening. The radio suddenly interrupts its normal broadcast. Stalin is dead. For my father, Stalin is God. We all hold our breath. We fear that this announcement might plunge him into such despair that he'll lose his mind. But he reacts with composure. The news is a lie, an imperialist plot, the ultimate and futile capitalist ploy. He scoffs at it.

For an entire, interminable night, my father is going to claim, against the whole world, that Stalin, his Stalin, is still alive.

The next morning, Radio Moscow confirms the news.

My father clasps his head in his hands, and he weeps.

He weeps for the rest of the day.

My sister takes advantage of the situation to go out.

Mama and I don't know what to do. We don't dare approach him, much less hug him. The choked sobs that escape from the chest of this man that we fear as we would a wild beast, these sobs seem so peculiar to us, so discordant, fed at the source by such an inscrutable sadness, that, far from feeling pity, we're frozen with fright and dumbstruck, as if witnessing a crime.

—◌—

Another memory comes to mind, Doctor, which, for some reason, I associate with this last one. Perhaps the two events took place in the same year?

I'm twelve. I've moved up into middle school. My teacher's name is Monsieur Verdier. I worship him. One day, he gives my mother a package. We open it, our hands trembling in anticipation. The package contains hand-me-downs from his son René, who is two years older than I. These clothes weren't sewn by hand like mine; rather, their tags show that they come from department stores. I'm dazzled by this sign of luxury. I try on the trousers. They're beautiful. They look good on me. My mother nudges me over to the mirror. I look at myself, pleased. I'm someone else. I'm rich. I stand up straight. The next day, I wear the trousers to school. At recess, the teacher's son comes over to me, looks me up and down with contempt, and slaps me, without a word. Right away, I make the connection between the slap and the package. From then on, I've been wary of gifts. I'm always waiting for the slap to follow.

That night, I'm feeling low. My father asks me why. I tell him. I still haven't learned to be on my guard. My father snaps back that I must have got what I deserved, that I surely committed a reprehensible act, an aggression of some kind. Or rather, no, I'm too spineless: some sneaky thing or other. He demands that I confess the misdeed. I tell him I didn't do anything wrong. What did you say? my father asks. I say nothing. I'm quaking all over now. Let's hear that again, screams my father. I didn't do anything wrong, I say, hiding my face behind a terrified arm.

He slaps me.

I believe that's the day, Doctor, when I became a criminal.

FIFTEEN

I READ.

I can't stop reading.

When I get home, it's hello, goodbye, and I shut myself up in the bedroom, flop down on the bed, toss to the floor the frilly pink kewpie doll my wife won at the fair (my reading inspires acts of violence), and I immerse myself in my book.

The next day, I start all over again.

One day in May, I'm sitting in the garden. I put on my glasses. I open my book. The birds are singing in the sky above and the leaves whisper in the trees, while the sun covers the slumbering landscape in golden gossamer. I'm joking, Monsieur Jean, just joking. I'm trying to get you to smile. You look so worried. Suddenly my wife comes running, casting terrified glances all about. What are the neighbors going to think? she murmurs. (My wife is obsessed by the idea of what the neighbors are going to think.)

What you have to realize, Monsieur Jean, is that out in the country, sitting in a garden is problematic. Reading there, worse still. But sitting there, reading a philosophy book is nothing short of scandalous.

The garden, you see, for country folks, is not that place cherished by poets where one gathers life's rosebuds all the livelong day, but the grounds for the most feverish, the most inhuman and the most mindless of activities. An inch-by-inch struggle against weeds that have never done us any harm—that's something beyond my comprehension. But this is no place to make light of the horticultural labor law.

Go back inside, my wife murmurs. Go back in, please.

I yield to her appeals. I get up, grudgingly. I drag my feet with the express purpose of showing my disagreement. In passing, I give a swift kick to one of the seven plaster dwarfs my wife has set around the garden to make it more cheery. Sneezy! cries my wife, her hands on her head. Before locking myself in the bedroom, I ask her in a firm voice to leave me the hell alone. Do not disturb please, I say. She's quite capable, under some false pretense, of opening the door with the sole purpose of catching me *flagrante delicto* in the act of daydreaming. I finally stretch out on the bed, diagonally (the greatest of my solitary pleasures), and I start reading a book that Molinier has lent me.

I read. I read. It's a vice. I read, goaded on by some compelling desire, some urge that's totally out of my control. I read as if my days were numbered, as if death awaited me that same day. I read happily. I read with delight. Have you noticed, Monsieur Jean, how polished my prose is since I've been in prison? Every day, through my reading, I discover the joys of thinking. For to read is to think. To read is my creed.

I read and reread the *Pensées*. I read and reread the *Correspondence*. Reading is the only happiness I know today. What I mean by that is, thanks to reading, my life, as hideous as it was, has now become, if not cheerful, then at least bearable. I made the decision, moreover, so as to better devote myself to reading, to sleep without my wife. I blamed it on insomnia, on my aching joints. My wife now sleeps on the couch in the living room.

As for me, I go to bed with my books.

Their company is, for the moment, the only one I tolerate.

My wife has grown jealous of them. On the evening to which I refer, she unscrews the lock on the bedroom door with a screwdriver, comes toward me with the look of a madwoman, tears off my glasses without a word, and stomps on them in a kind of rage. Glasses that cost over a thousand francs.

I hit her. On principle.

You ask me, Monsieur Jean, whether reading can make us better people?

A vast question that I couldn't begin to answer.

Which one of Pascal's *Pensées,* you ask, is my favorite of all?

My preference has shifted over time. Prior to my detention, the *Pensée* where Pascal asserts that all the unhappiness of men arises from one single fact, that they cannot stay quietly in their own chamber—that *Pensée* I found deeply affecting, and I made it my own, to the point where I at times seriously considered going into seclusion.

But ever since that act, which certain people have called a crime, but which I personally look upon as an act of pure logic; in other words, ever since I've been shut up in my cell, I have been irritated by this sentence. It seems to attest to a rejection of men and the world, motivated by fear and caution far more than by courage. And now that fate has sequestered me within these four walls, I'm inclined to think, Monsieur Jean, that all the unhappiness of man arises, on the contrary, from his being enclosed, enclosed in his mother's lap, thoroughly caught up in his passion to restrain his mind, the willing inmate of his own little portable prison, and of others far larger that he shares with the rest of the livestock.

The *Pensée* that I have most often quoted?

In the interest of satisfying my clientele, I try, during each visit, to make the requisite reference to the thinking reed. We guides know perfectly well that our customers love to hear stories they already know. And this thinking reed business, well, everyone in France knows it. Or almost everyone.

I must confess, to my great shame, that I had never heard the story of the thinking reed when I first started out. When I came across it in the ten-page brochure that Monsieur Molinier gave me, back when I was first hired, I had absolutely no idea what it meant. I simply could not connect this little phrase to anything sensible whatsoever. I imagined a man, I imagined a reed, I sometimes imagined a lanky man waving back and forth like a reed, or I imagined a reed with a man's head (which struck me as highly comical), but I couldn't conceive of why this phrase, as Monsieur Molinier used to emphasize, had come down to us over four centuries and had spread to the four corners of the earth. Am I dumber than the rest, I wondered anxiously?

Since Monsieur Molinier had encouraged us, at one of our locker room meetings, to include in the regular routine some musings of our own, provided, he hastened to add, that they not stray too far from the spirit of the text, I pondered long and hard over the famous phrase: Man is a thinking reed.

I began by reading the entire *Pensée*. For it cannot be understood, Monsieur Jean, unless read from start to finish.

Yes, Monsieur Jean. I know it by heart. Man is but a reed, the most feeble thing in nature; but he is a thinking reed. The entire universe need not arm itself to crush him. A vapor, a drop of water suffices to kill him. But, if the universe were to crush him, man would still be more noble than that which killed him, because he knows that he dies and the advantage that the universe has over him; the universe knows nothing of this.

As you might well imagine, I'm not so foolish as to indulge in textual analysis in front of my visitors, however much I would like to. Everyone abhors textual analysis, it's a well-known fact. French teachers are the only ones who haven't figured that out, as they pursue their heavy-handed commentary, when the lightest touch would suffice. Still, I do try to get my visitors to reflect, as I myself did.

So, one day, emboldened by a fresh bout of reading, I decide to give it a try. I'm to serve as guide to a group of grief counselors trained to treat victims of misfortune, who appear innocuous, or even simple-minded, and ready to swallow just about anything. I seize the opportunity. I prepare myself. I clear my throat. Since they claim to provide some consolation to the wretched, let them begin, I reason, by reflecting upon what constitutes both the cause of misfortune and its remedy.

Death is the most fairly distributed thing in the world, I tell them. A nice preamble. The dignity of man, I say to them, is in the fact that he thinks, and that he thinks he is mortal. It is because man knows he is mortal that he thinks, I say. I place heavy emphasis on man's finite nature. In man's nature, fundamentally, there is nothing but death. Every man, I tell them, is a dead man on a spree. He's born. He makes his way. And in the twinkling of an eye, it's over. A feast for worms. I feel inspired. Relaxed. Happy days, Blaise! Death needs to be nurtured. It must be pampered, like love. It takes no less than a lifetime to fashion a quality death. But who takes a quality death seriously these days? Who takes it seriously, apart from a few African potentates? Such an idea makes people laugh.

But not me.

That evening, Monsieur Molinier reprimands me, in front of Turpin and Musto, who pretend not to hear him. It's the first time Monsieur Molinier has reprimanded me. It's made me upset. Turpin brushes his uniform, while Musto wipes off the table where we've just had our coffee. (That task always falls to Musto. Neither Turpin nor I would wipe the table, for all the money in the world.)

Our visitors, Monsieur Molinier sermonizes, have no desire to spend their Sunday getting bummed out. (Monsieur Molinier enjoys using terms like *bummed out* to prove he's attuned to young, eclectic youth culture, that he wasn't schooled among dusty tomes alone, but in the rough-and-tumble of real life.) Eschatology, my dear fellow, is not meant to interest the general public. Musto raises his head, dumbfounded. Eschatology? People don't come here to be told horrible things. Which is perfectly understandable, you have to admit.

To this, I retort (to myself) with two points: first, that I don't much care for the term *bummed out;* and second, that talking about death doesn't strike me as crude, much less a subject of affliction or horror. Not that I find it charming, but death simply doesn't scare me. Perhaps it's because I lack imagination. Or because I don't exist.

Back home, I'm on edge.

I get blamed for something.

I explode.

I don't give a damn about dust on the furniture. I don't give a damn about the mess and I don't give a damn about any of this household crap. So just leave me alone, will you?

Christ!

Don't you understand, I say to my wife, that our dignity resides in thinking, and not in waxing the furniture?

She stares at me, stunned.

And mainly in thinking about death, I shout.

But men loathe thinking, and they rush around all day just to keep from thinking (I'm venting my pent-up anger that I've been holding in since this morning). All the powders and greasepaint they slather over their lives, all their brainless novels, all their acrobatics, the purpose of all that is to keep them from thinking, I yell, and with an angry sweep of the arm, I knock over the collection of dolls lined up on the sideboard.

Not so loud, says my wife.

The sole purpose, I shout.

My wife rushes to the windows and slams them shut.

And the sole purpose of work is to keep them from thinking, I shout.

So, the sole purpose of everything we do in the world is to keep us from thinking, my wife snaps back.

Voilà! I say.

That's absurd, says my wife.

That's the way it is, I say.

So, if you take it a step further, thinking about all that also keeps you from thinking, says my wife.

Of course, I say, evasively.

You drive me insane, screams my wife.

A good start, I say.

He's at it again, says my wife with a sigh.

Hence it is that men have such love of sound and fury that they beg for turmoil.

I said not so loud, says my wife.

Men refuse to think that they'll croak someday, I continue, though I, for one, think about it all the time.

My poor darling, cries my wife, flinging herself at me by hugging me against her abundant flesh.

I'm tempted to take a little nap in this cushiony bed suddenly offered to me, but now is no time for weakness.

O *ridicolosissimo eroe,* I say contemptuously. And at that, an expression of such incredulity appears on my wife's face that I can't refrain from bursting out in laughter.

May I note, in this regard, that the issue of laughter is a constant preoccupation of mine. Ever since my thoughts have turned toward the things of this world—in other words, ever since I became intelligent (for intelligence is not a quality of the mind but a particular way it has of orienting itself)—as I was saying, ever since I began thinking, I've been discovering that all things are worthy of thought, laughter just like all the rest. Does laughter deserve a rightful place in the life of the mind, or not? This query, which undoubtedly seems commonplace in the eyes of a serious thinker, is for me of great concern. Especially since I have not thus far come across a single mention of laughter in my readings of Pascal. And no matter how hard I scrutinize the portraits of the great man, I detect no penchant whatsoever for laughing.

Though the smile on his death mask could well indicate the repression of an enormous outburst of laughter. A repression powerful enough to be fatal. But I'm not certain of my interpretation and, for the moment, I'm keeping it to myself. Otherwise, people are going to start thinking again that I'm out of control.

You hope that I'm not going to lose it in your absence, Monsieur Jean? What do you mean by that?

You're going to go away for a month?

To the shore?

To go sailing?

That's simply horrible!

For me, Monsieur Jean, hell is precisely that: at sea in the dark of night, with one abyss above and one abyss below.

Sixteen

At what point did Molinier's aloofness start making itself felt? I'd be at pains to say exactly when, Your Honor.

Maybe back in June, with the visit of the freshman class from Lycée Blaise-Pascal in Clermont-Ferrand.

At first glance, the incident seems trivial. That day, the students of the freshman class from Lycée Blaise-Pascal in Clermont-Ferrand await me in the museum lobby. I don't like freshmen, Your Honor. And truth be told, I don't like young people. They depress me. Those little creatures, all anxious about sex, those little bits of unfinished womanhood, those nubile teases with their pointy rear ends—I can't stand them, there's no other way of putting it. And their affectations, their wiggling about, their gnat-like restlessness—it all gets on my nerves. Just looking at them makes me seethe with anger. Let Turpin or Musto handle them, anybody else but me. Not me.

No thanks.

I'm a guide, granted, but not a guide for the young: no, no, no. It's simple: I loathe young people. They say that today's youth is brainless. It was ever thus. When it comes to civility, zero. Horrendous manners. And no virtue. Nothing straightforward. Devious and evasive. Take the nail-studded belt. They could laugh at it outright. Laugh to their heart's delight. But no. They're all stifled giggles, sneaky shyness, mealy expressions and hypocritically bowed heads. So what does all this have to do with Pascal and literature . . . Excuse me, Your Honor, but if you keep interrupting me, I'll never finish.

So, with my body moving forward and my spirit held back, I make my way to the lobby where the students are waiting. My dragging feet alone prove how disinclined I am to serve as their guide. I'll be present only in the flesh, I say to myself. It's a little exercise, Your Honor, which I have come to perfect.

Silence, I say, icily. And I wait for silence to prevail. If I can't overawe children, whom can I overawe?

Once the troops are reduced to silence, I undertake to deliver an exordium on the pedagogical principles advocated by the Gentlemen of Port-Royal. Those in charge of education, I venture, would stand to gain a great deal by drawing inspiration from the following principles: one, gain custody of the children as soon as they are weaned. Two, keep constant watch on them, even in their sleep, so as to prevent the incursions of vice. For vice is swift, while virtue is slow. Three—silence, I said—three, forbid daydreaming and idleness, those malevolent seeds of illicit desires. Four, suppress face powder, lipstick, earrings and artificially curled hair, which, as we know, are the lure of Satan. Suppress any outlandish manner of dress that tends toward the infinitely small. Ban brainless babble bearing on boobs (no one laughs). Five, have them alternate unrelentingly between work and prayer. Until they drop. And penance for the slightest lapse.

The democratically-minded teachers glare at me disapprovingly.

I then march them along to the Painting Gallery. I'm still feeling as ill-disposed toward them as before. I therefore limit myself to pointing to the paintings as I read out the titles: *The Crucifixion* by Philippe de Champaigne, *Ecce Homo,* by the same, *Saint John the Baptist* (his head on a platter, Your Honor, like a common chicken thigh), attributed to the seventeenth century Spanish school, and the portrait of Pascal by Quesnel, looking exactly like Daniel Mesguich, Your Honor. You've never heard of that actor? You should get out more often, Your Honor. And while my body is heading toward the Manuscript Gallery, I ask myself this question: Mother looks like Pascal, Pascal looks like Daniel Mesguich, so does Mother look like Daniel Mesguich? No.

In the Manuscript Gallery, I'm as expeditious as can be. I confine myself to reading, without the least comment, this *Pensée,* which I cherish despite its abstruseness: "The power of flies; they win battles, hinder our soul from acting, consume our body."

Upon which, I remain silent for over five minutes.

Before departing, the democratically-minded teachers go complain to Monsieur Molinier. They are quite shaken.

Monsieur Molinier promptly summons me. It's the first time I've ever been in his office. Have a seat. Thank you, sir. This is no time to be calling him Jacques. I notice on his desk the photograph of a woman whose face is burdened with large, heavy-framed glasses that overpower her features.

Monsieur Molinier behaves like someone truly in charge, something I will never know how to do. Lips pinched, firmly determined, he's on the attack from the outset. Your behavior, my dear fellow, is unacceptable. Unacceptable. One would think you derived pleasure from disheartening the customers. You're gloomy. If not to say macabre. He says this without raising his voice, as do eminent personages when they aim to wound.

But sir, I retort, this isn't exactly the Moulin Rouge we're operating here, is it?

That's precisely what it is, he snaps back, reestablishing the hierarchy. Our customers, however educated, come here to have a good time. First and foremost. And you would do well to help them achieve that objective. This is a piece of advice. He continues, sententiously: the respect of the customer, the transmission of culture, our role as guide, spiritual guide . . . spiritual guide, Your Honor; doesn't that ring a bell?

I swallow all this without a word, but suddenly, I start sneezing uncontrollably.

In order to give you the most accurate picture of myself (for, if I want to be understood by the jury, I must give the most accurate picture possible; you said so yourself), let me make mention, Your Honor, that I am subject to sneezing fits on a regular basis. The more I've thought about this disruptively noisy condition, which has the disadvantage of attracting attention to my humble self, I've concluded that it's a kind of oblique protest, an inopportune way of opposing what I consider an aggression, as I'm far too timorous to do so in words. Not a very endearing condition, either, eliciting negligible sympathy, unlike digestive ailments, which are universally appreciated, among the female population in particular, for the influence they exert on affairs of the heart.

It's just that the nose, throughout history, has never acquired the nobility of the eyes, the eroticism of the mouth, or the abundant force of the large intestine. It is and remains an instrument that is not only useless (it always seems unseemly to make use of it), but cumbersome (I'm thinking of my own, which is long and pitiable, like my dick, which is long and pitiable, my neck, which is long and pitiable, and like my whole body, which is long and pitiable, and which is more likely to elicit rejection in all its guises than spontaneous friendliness).

At the risk of being taken for a scoundrel, I must add another descriptive feature if I'm to appear in my truest light: I enjoy playing the bully and constantly feigning ill will. Through these exercises in nastiness at which I excel, and which the female population finds terribly attractive (especially social workers), I appease the urge for provocation that I still occasionally experience; but most importantly, thanks to this ruse, I dissimulate the even more repugnant feelings that I harbor in secret, those I couldn't possibly avow, for fear of being seen as a monster.

I'll stop the self-mockery here, Your Honor. A complete inventory of my faults and shortcomings would amount to an enormous enterprise. I'd never finish. And it's liable to do me harm.

Having proven that he was the undisputed master, and that he had established his dominion over me without resistance (what fools men are!), Monsieur Molinier relaxes. He takes off his glasses (suddenly revealing two tiny, expressionless eyes) and wipes them with a chamois cloth that he carefully removes from his pocket.

He asks how my reading is coming along, and without waiting for an answer: What irks me about Pascal, don't you see, is his holier-than-thou side.

Now hold on, you imbecile, not so fast. I say: Hold it right there! My sneezing fit stops dead. Your vision, sir, is far too simplistic. I'm afraid you have no right. It's by just such reductionism that bodies of work get distorted beyond recognition and dismissed forever. If my memory serves me, Pascal writes the following: It is incomprehensible that God should exist, and incomprehensible that He should not. It's not at all the same thing, now, is it? Let's not get carried away! Pascal is straddling, rather uncomfortably, that infernal paradox without attempting to resolve it through some ruse: incomprehensible that God should exist, and incomprehensible that He should not.

Likewise, I say (I don't know what's come over me, phrases are springing to my lips without the least resistance), likewise, Pascal asserts that the world is everything, and that the world is nothing. The world is nothing, I say, because the world is depraved, because the world is vile, because it is black with blood and swarming with flies, which amounts to saying that it doesn't exist. But at the same time, it is everything, because it is all that man knows, the place where he can love and hope, with an incorrigible hopefulness, that good shall triumph and happiness shall prevail.

Pascal is searching, far beyond ordinary existence, beyond the dogmas and the herds, a crystal core, hard and glistening, that no evil could corrupt. But this crystal does not exist, Pascal knows this, and this leaves him inconsolable, utterly inconsolable. For although he concedes that it is foolish and illusory to want to change the world, something compelling within urges him not to flee from it.

Thus, he says yes to this world, and he says no. On the one hand, Mademoiselle Roannez and the pleasures of conversation, money and sinecures, fools who claim to soar with the eagles, life as a permanent cabaret; on the other, excruciating solitude and castigation, the crushing silence of nothingness, the spirit that opens up to God, and God fails to appear. Which

143

to choose? Pascal does not choose. It's foolish to choose. Pascal says yes and no at the same time. Both yes and no, for he scorns the middle-of-the-road (the other name for mediocrity), for he despises compromise (the very idea makes him faint), for, as he says, there is no middle ground between heaven and earth (the mean is never golden), for the universe has no center, or else the center is everywhere. I pause to catch my breath.

And if we carefully scrutinize Pascal's death mask, we can clearly observe, I say, that at the fateful hour, his face is saying yes while his body says no. Finally, Pascal can say yes and no in the same breath, yes and no in the same instant. Hence his uncanny smile, discreetly triumphant, which still haunts me.

Monsieur Molinier stares at me with such an astounded expression that I can't help laughing to myself.

I must insist on pointing out, at this juncture, for those who are not fortunate enough to know me, that I'm not as sinister as Monsieur Molinier claims. I can on occasion make facetious remarks and encourage the visitors to crack jokes, even though my heart, as the saying goes, is not in it. Whenever I cite Pascal's spiritual director, a certain Singlin, I always mark a deliberate pause. The Earth being populated by a considerable number of idiots, there is unfailingly one person in every group who will launch into "Singlin in the Rain," and cause a commotion. So, despite my inner disapproval, I display a discreet smile, and assume an amused and sardonic air. I've observed, moreover, that such an attitude substantially enhances my earnings in tips.

I could say a lot, Your Honor, on the topic of tipping. The first remark that we guides can make is that tips in no way reward the quality, the flair, the imagination or the erudition of our services; rather, they are directly proportional to the number of clichés, coarse laughter, winks, nudges, and lewd jokes we reel off per minute, and I'm only slightly exaggerating. To declare, for instance, with a sly grin, that man is a thinking reed, only when he's not a drinking reed, or to call Pascal "the Whipping Boy," following Musto's example, automatically triggers merriment among the visitors, merriment that unfailingly translates into bigger tips.

I, for one, refuse to call Pascal "the Whipping Boy." There's no way on earth I would call Pascal "the Whipping Boy." To make a little extra cash, I prefer making fun of the portraits of the nuns, who are all ugly as sin. There's a little fun I have regularly with the Germans that is almost always a winner. Even though it pains me, I stand before the portrait of Mère Angélique, and I declare: Ve vill now zee dis schöne Frau, ya? Works like a charm.

Excuse me?

No, Your Honor, I'm not concerned. I trust Molinier. Far be it from me to predict what's to come.

Then, there's the dinner Molinier organizes in my honor with our two spouses, one as inept as the other. So there I am, playing the scholar, enjoying it to the hilt, with Pascal this, and Pascal that. And Molinier upping the ante with Blaise this and Blaise that, and don't you think the sexual repression present in Pascal's correspondence with Mademoiselle Roannez seems blah blah blah, and isn't the connection between Lautréamont and Pascal blah blah blah. Meanwhile, my wife is watching me closely to learn the refined way to eat her melon. And I'm in the clouds somewhere: Lautréamont, Ah! Lautréamont, I'll have to read his poetry one of these days. And he says, Indispensable, my boy. And I come back with: don't you feel that Pascal somehow substitutes the horror of the physical void for the horror of the metaphysical void? And he says, looking intense, doesn't Pascal's influence on Guy Debord seem crucial? And I say, Guy Debord? And he says, the greatest of this century, my good fellow, the one and only. And our two spouses, bored stiff, left out, unhappy. And my wife, eyeing me once more to figure out how to use her fish knife. Meanwhile, I'm completely oblivious. And Molinier is also becoming irritated. So, to loosen things up a bit, I go say: My friend, Pascal wrote that true eloquence cares not for eloquence, and that true morality cares not for morality. Could we not add that true literature cares not for literature, and that real life cares not for life? Ah, ah, ah! And now Molinier's growing seriously glum, really annoyed, and there's his final remark as we take leave. And my repartee, tit for tat: But I'm not trying to pit myself against anyone at all, sir, other than myself. And Molinier's utterly furious, but I can't stop myself now. Words, words, words. Words until the head spins. Words ad nauseam. Spiraling sentences, sentences that suck you in like black holes, sentences one utters without thinking, without meaning to, and which later prove decisive, probably because they were telling the truth. So, to cut me short, Molinier chimes in with: I who am a great expert on Pascal . . . And my instant rejoinder: Do you want people to think well of you? Then don't speak. Livid, Molinier says, how dare you? And I say, it's a quote. From Pascal. And I take my leave.

I'll pay for that.

No, nothing more serious, Your Honor, I can't think of anything more serious than that to report.

You absolutely cannot comprehend the reasons that drove me to this murder. Do we ever understand them, Your Honor?

I get the feeling that the more I talk, the deeper I descend into a well of mystery.

Could I be insane, perhaps?

Seventeen

It's war, sir. It's war. Molinier is avoiding me. He's giving me the cold shoulder. He keeps me at arm's length with icy hellos and even icier how-are-things. And if I address him, he pretends to be elsewhere: did you say something? The favor he showed me in the early days has now vanished. No more friendly pats on the back, no more "my boy," isn't that so, my boy, might I suggest, my boy, that you read, no more "Just call me Jacques" whispered in my ear, no more gift books with passages underlined in red, remarkable stuff, boy, remarkable, a must-read, no more infinite commentaries on the infinite, on the madness of Port-Royal, not a word, no more soaring heights, no more anything. We remain desperately riveted to the ground, loathing one another.

From now on, when Monsieur Molinier addresses me, it's to cross-examine me, and I mean cross-examine, on the life and work of Blaise Pascal, like a chemistry professor, sir, on test day, like . . . I didn't dare say it, sir, but like a judge, splitting hairs, with the sole purpose of finding me in error.

You don't know Blaise's astrological sign, do you? he queries, point-blank. I say nothing. I've resolved, despite all the respect due him, not to reply. Turpin's advice leads me to do so—he thinks I overdo it. By that, I suppose he means that I read too much, talk too much, in short, that I exist too much, and should go back to being more inconspicuous. Blaise's astrological sign? I don't flinch. But Monsieur Molinier is hardheaded. He rephrases his question. I hold my ground. He persists. I do the same. He comes at me again. Once, twice. Come on, now, you know it: is Pascal Sagittarius or Pisces? He's grinning malevolently. Pascal was born the nineteenth of June. I remember that because Mother's birthday falls on a seventeenth, but I'd rather die than reply to this kind of inanity. I hold my tongue. He's hounding now. What does he want from me? He's got the mulishness of a detective who thinks he's got his man. And the same method, too. He won't let up until he's wrested a few words out of me. Maybe it's in July, I end up saying. For I always end up by giving in. Both parties breathe easier.

This situation is excruciating for me, sir, and I don't know how to get Molinier to see reason. I honestly thought that he would grant me, if not friendship, then at least treatment as an equal, thanks to which we might have been able to reconsider literature and the world. Fool that I was! It's turned out to be just the reverse. Monsieur Molinier looks down on me. With that annoyed concern that a boss shows toward the underlings they can't do without, but who, for unspeakable reasons, have become abhorrent to him.

I'm deeply sorry about all of this, sir. I'd found a port at Port-Royal-des-Champs. It provided the circumstances best suited to regulating my life, a form of serenity, a peace and freedom that it would cost me dearly to abandon.

I search with my soul to understand the reasons for this reversal. But for the moment, they remain unfathomable. What have I done? What crime have I committed? What secret purpose does he hope to achieve by harassing me relentlessly? I'm adrift in conjecture.

Why does he lie in wait like that for me to make a blunder? Why do my answers offend him so? What is there in my attitude that is so reprehensible? Have I somehow offended him unintentionally? Is Monsieur Molinier afraid of losing the upper hand? Does he think I'm trying to take his place? But I have no ambitions for promotion, I don't give a damn about promotions, and he knows it.

Is he unhappy or dissatisfied with my work, but afraid to say so? On that point, I'm adamant. I think of myself as an excellent guide, owing to the uncanny concurrence between the special attributes required of the job, and the salient features of my character. My laziness, (which is not a natural laziness, as one might suspect, but the result, I dare say, of an enormous effort on my part), my fondness of disguise, my deep interest in the dead and in martyrology, my proclivity for teaching, all combine to make me an outstanding guide.

Is he expecting a *mea culpa* from me? But for what fault? It's utterly maddening. Had I been wrong about him from the start? Could it be he's a real bastard? A real son of a bitch? A petty tyrant without knowing it?

Should I ascribe the annoyance I cause him to some jealousy or other? Or is there some unintelligible slight, a secret humiliation that I unknowingly arouse in him, and which I must discover at all costs before the situation breaks down further and becomes unbearable?

Faced with this dizzying onslaught of questions, I am gripped by anxiety, whose center is everywhere and its circumference nowhere. Especially at night, sir, when fear lurks in the gloom, and life's big questions rise to the surface, in funereal procession.

One evening, as I'm having trouble falling asleep, I start

reading a book that Monsieur Molinier lent me a few months ago, but which I've disregarded until now. (I opted instead for a well-documented work on the bombing of Pearl Harbor.) The author's name is Montaigne, and I know he fascinated Pascal. I open it. I read through a few lines. They seem unintelligible to me. I close the book. Sleep eludes me still. So I pick up the discarded book once more, and I land on this sentence: Princes give me much if they take nothing from me, and do me much good when they do me no harm. Herein is the exact formulation of the behavior I would hope for in a master. That he take nothing from me and that he do me no harm; that's all I expect from him.

But Monsieur Molinier is no prince. He's a servant who fancies himself a prince. And presently, he's picking a quarrel with me. And he is destroying my peace of mind.

I'm dying daily to tell him I deem his behavior exceedingly common, exceedingly petty, and that, when all is said and done, he's acting like a little culture cop. I'd be so relieved.

I've decided, nevertheless, to keep my mouth shut. Not rush into anything. Wait for better days. It's the reasonable thing to do. But Molinier has to stop nitpicking. Otherwise . . .

Need I confess, nevertheless, that I have the impression, in the middle of this war, that I am in a way more at peace?

Eighteen

You need some evidence?

Significant factors from my childhood?

But how, Your Honor, shall I choose from the chaotic stockpile of my memories the one that will speak of me most truthfully? How shall I convey to you what's essential if I don't know myself? How shall I render for you the things that have affected and wounded me since birth?

I would have preferred, for this, our last interview, to tell you about the gym class where, having suddenly realized that my underwear was dirty, I stubbornly refused to stand up, and sat obstinately immobile on the locker room bench during the entire workout, while the tracksuit-clad instructor shouted, in exasperation: What's the matter with you, you little moron? Hey, what's wrong with this little shit? How much longer are you going to play dead? Move your ass, for Christ's sake, believing he'd detected, in the shame that was literally paralyzing me, some insubordinate act.

I would have liked to speak to you about shame.

I would have liked to describe for you the imitation leather jacket made by my mother, which I took off without her knowing and hid in the bottom of my book bag, out of shame.

I blush at the very thought of it now.

I would have liked to recall more vividly the leafless garden full of abandoned garden tools and dreary rubble, with the outhouse in the far corner where I would fear to venture after nightfall.

I would have liked to summon up for you, prevailing over my embarrassment, the dimly lit, cramped two-room apartment that I never allowed a single friend to enter, the old wood-burning stove in the corner, the cold water sink where we would take turns washing in icy water, my father first, at six A.M., my sister and I next, shivering, and last, Mama, finally free of us.

I would have liked to tell you what an ordeal each meal together was. It was our hatred that we wolfed down together.

I would have liked to move you to pity with the death of my cat Rags, who used to sleep every night nuzzled against my shoulder, and whom my father bludgeoned to death with a hoe for stealing a slice of ham.

My father, Your Honor, didn't like thieves.

My father didn't like cowards.

Nor did he like those he called parasites. Is that what his children were for him?

I learned later, much later, that he had abandoned a wife and child in Spain in 1939, without ever contacting them again. I envied them.

I would have liked to confide in you, as in a sister, my dread of days off that meant our father would be at home all day, glued to his Teppaz radio, listening to the triumphant voices of Radio Moscow and the impassioned speeches of Stalin, imposing upon us absolute silence, forcing us to remain as motionless as cadavers.

I would have liked to talk to you, Your Honor, about this notion that slowly took shape in my mind, frightening at first, then gradually mundane and familiar, that my father was, in a way, a fiendish figure, the incarnation of Evil, whose presence wreaked upon his family nothing but shame and despair.

I would have liked to tell you, Your Honor . . .

Nineteen

And I, whom all spirit of disorderly conduct had long since abandoned, I now secretly await the opportunity to hasten events. To cause an outrage. To send everything flying. To be done with it, Doctor, once and for all. Because sooner or later, this situation has to come to an end. It has to end, Doctor, before I do something I might regret.

One afternoon, we're playing dominos while waiting for the coach full of British retirees scheduled to arrive at 3 o'clock. Double six. Double naught. Musto cares less about winning than about joking around and having a laugh. Which I find infuriating. I tell him as much. He's angered. I shout. Terrible things. It's right before Christmas, and I'm feeling very anxious. I'm always anxious, Doctor, right before Christmas. The words that somewhere deep down I intend for Molinier get hurled straight into Musto's face. Lackey, I call him, wimp, jerk, phony. Measly little cop, I say. Measly little culture cop.

All the insults I've hoarded over a month against that schmuck Molinier, I hurl them straight at Musto. Unspeakable conduct, yes, Doctor, I admit. Musto puts on his usual sad-eyed spaniel look. I can't stand his sad-eyed spaniel look. It sets me off again. Turpin and Molinier intervene. Turpin comes right up to me. Gets in my face. I don't like people getting in my face. I can smell his breath. It stinks of stale beer. Who do you think you are, Turpin says; you think you're better than us, or what? It's not just because you read all those . . . You can just shut up, all right? I scream. Now I'm really letting loose. Turpin backs off. I exit, without once looking back. I stride toward the parking lot. I get into my VW. I start the engine. Black birds slam into a concrete sky and drop, stunned. The whore has parked her van in its regular spot, and is reading a love story while she waits for truckers to unzip for a fast one. Her lime-green eyelids and cheeks garishly plastered with rouge make her look like a Brazilian parrot. She's got a cigarette in her mouth for practice, ha ha ha, sorry, Doctor, I'm tense, I'm seething, I feel like exploding, spouting nonsense. Being locked up doesn't agree with me, actually.

And the more insight I gain into my soul, the more the world around me shifts and darkens. At the museum, the atmosphere is sinister. Monsieur Molinier, who finally understood that I'm weary of Byzantine arguments over Pascal and Port-Royal, has practically ceased to speak to me at all. Turpin is aloof. And Musto, ever since our quarrel, refuses to take on all the housekeeping chores by himself. He sulks.

I no longer go to the locker room at lunchtime or at closing. I have no desire to chat. In fact, with the passage of time, I talk less and less. My ideal is to be as laconic as my cat. One meow for my ration of food. Another for my ravings. Another, perhaps, to express dissent, though I'm not sure. It doesn't matter, in the end, whether I express my dissent. Barring exceptional circumstances.

At noon, I go to the park and sit on a bench and put my lunchbox next to me. Above the bench, a sign hanging from a tree trunk reads:

—∾—

This park is under your stewardship.
Do not walk on the grass.
Do not pick flowers.
Do not break tree branches.

—∾—

I added, in pencil, and in tiny print: *Do not follow the guide, he doesn't know where he's going.*

The weather's getting colder, so it seems. But I've grown indifferent to the cold. As to everything else. I keep a flask of bourbon in my pocket at all times. I take a swig, then a second, then a third, then sometimes a fourth. Afterward, I feel much better. My mind is at once sharper and more measured. It's an odd thing. At two o'clock, I take my place in the lobby where I await the tourists. I feel slightly tipsy. If Musto and Turpin cross my path, I turn my head so as not to notice them.

Visitors have grown scarce. All we get now are pimply students in the throes of sexual upheaval who make themselves sick writing abstruse dissertations on the works of Pascal, or a few fanatics who've spent ages researching some topic as obscure as it is useless, wandering around in circles and getting nowhere. This group represents a real threat for museum guides like us. For their erudition competes directly with ours, exposing ours for what it really is: shallow and showy.

I've resumed my philosophical sessions at the café des Platanes, as well as my strolls along country roads. There are days when I cover over twenty kilometers on foot.

Even I don't quite grasp what leads me to drive myself to exhaustion in this way. I harbor no particular love of nature. And when I do observe it, I'm overcome by an uneasy feeling of silence and melancholy.

What's more, I'm fully opposed to physical exercise. It embitters me.

And then, I confess, nature frightens me. I'm more afraid of barnyard dogs than I am of the beasts of the forest, though less than I am of farmers. I can't stand birds, which I like only when cooked, and all that greenery makes me nauseous.

Nor do I excel at introspective probing, which is said to benefit greatly from stirring the calf muscles. Such probing exercises, it seems to me, always involve those who are dirty-minded and moody, the self-absorbed, who seek only to gaze into the corruption of their own hearts, to wallow in it like swine, to foment fresh emotional crises that will cause them dreadful suffering, but which will serve to fill the vacuum of their existence.

Nature does not inspire me, reveals nothing to me, teaches me nothing. Could the example of the hare, the doe and other animals intended for the hunt equip me for life's struggles? Does the countryside expand my vision of the human species? No, no, no. You see nothing but Whites there. Never, never a black face, never a yellow face or a mulatto.

Nevertheless, the countryside does present one inestimable advantage: I can soliloquize in peace.

I soliloquize, then. I speak to myself for days on end.

About everything. About nothing. About the twelve francs I owe Turpin. About my right hand pocket: well, I'll be damned, it's all unstitched. About good and evil. I talk to myself about good and evil. And whenever I talk to myself about good and evil, there inevitably comes the moment when I think about Mama.

—∞—

One day, Doctor, Molinier comes to let me know that a busload of Portuguese Pinto Bank employees has arrived. They can go to hell. I say those precise words: They-can-go-to-hell. I feel my soul filled with knightly honor. Molinier becomes livid. Very well. You'll be hearing from me about this. And he turns and leaves, walking with tiny, cautious steps, as if the ground were littered with landmines.

I settle onto my park bench. I sense I'm experiencing a crucial moment of my life, Doctor. And yet, I feel nothing. You've been to the barbershop, Doctor. That haircut makes you look younger. At six, Monsieur Molinier is standing stock still near the ticket window, waiting for me. The look on his face is frightening. These are distressing circumstances which . . . I don't let him complete his sentence. You're dismissing me, and I'm thrilled. I had been wishing, as it happened, to take some time to reflect upon a certain number of subjects. I plan to undertake a reading of Pascal's commentators, whose names I've drawn up on a list. Here are the titles, Doctor; I always keep this list with me:

—∞—

Albert Béguin: *Pascal*

Gilberte Périer: *The Life of Monsieur Pascal*

Sainte-Beuve: *Port-Royal*

Léon Brunschvicg: *The Genius of Pascal; Pascal; Pascal and Descartes, Readers of Montaigne*

Henry Lefebvre: *Pascal*

Louis Lafuma: *Pascalian Controversies*

Georges Brunet: *Pascal's Wager; A Supposed Treatise of Pascal; The Discourse on Passion and Love*

Lucien Goldman: *The Hidden God*

J. Mesnard: *Pascal and the Roannez Family*

—∞—

Back home, I don't say anything to my wife. I dread her lamentations.

The next day, I get up at the regular time. I shave and dress, as if I were going to work. I go out, and take the path leading into the oak grove. I walk for a long while. I look for a dry place. I stretch out under an oak tree. I watch the clouds move across the sky. I think about nothing. I feel fine.

I've noticed, in passing, that since I've had the leisure for it, I've been spending less time reading. I've not yet begun reading Pascal's commentators, and it's unlikely I ever will. If I happen to purchase a newspaper, it's only to wrap my sandwich in, or to wipe myself.

I still carry my flask of bourbon with me. Never do I leave the house without it. I take several swigs. It cheers me up. Almost. When I get back home, I tell my wife all the incidents that have punctuated my day. I tell her the episode of the drunken rugbymen and my terrifying tirade. She doesn't think it's funny. But I roar with laughter.

I can't say why, but I can put up with my wife more easily now that I've begun lying to her. Her rebukes annoy me less. Her complaints annoy me less. And her perpetual stomachaches hardly annoy me anymore at all.

In fact, I no longer think about running away, as I so often planned before. As recently as a few months ago, I was laying out my get-away plans, poring over atlases in secret; euphoric, I think about how I would take the bus into the city, sleep at the Hôtel du Centre, near the McDonald's, in a single room that looked out onto a featureless wall. I've dumped her, I would say to myself as I fell asleep, cold-hearted. But in the morning, already dispirited by the city's gloom, tormented at the idea that my wife, sick with worry, had telephoned all the police stations in the county to turn up some trace of me, road-weary before the journey had even begun, I would set out pathetically on my return trip home.

I'm gauging how easy it is to lie to and mislead those who think they know us. And how easy it is to lie to oneself. For my father did kill my mother, of that I am convinced. I have no more doubts about the awful conjecture I had been sketching out for months. My mother died of the sorrow my father caused her.

Twenty

THERE IS ONE AREA, DOCTOR, WHERE I NEED TO BE EXTRA careful if I'm not to attract my wife's attention, and that's to make sure I keep the days of the week straight. I sometimes get confused, and think it's Sunday, when it's already Monday.

I spend the majority of my time in the oak grove. Which, for me, amounts to staying home in my room, since I never cross paths with a single human being, and I'm never disturbed there. I'm getting used to the noises of the woods. They no longer frighten me. The more time I spend there, in fact, the less fear I feel. Occasionally, I'll cry out for no particular reason. It doesn't trouble any of the animals.

My woodland excursions feature only one drawback. They leave traces of mud that require explaining away upon my return home. In other words, I have to lie. Lying wears me down.

One evening, I get lost in the oak grove. I walk in circles. I come back to where I started. Daylight is starting to wane.

It takes me hours to find my way out. It's pitch black by the time I find the road. Barnyard dogs howl as I pass. A woman is sitting on her doorstep. She's filthy. She's fat. She looks half asleep. She's falling into the arms of death, I think to myself. What time is it? When I get back home, my wife has block-aded all entryways, and has barricaded the door with the table and chairs. She greets me with an ominous face. I will learn from her later that, racked with worry, she phoned Monsieur Molinier, who sounded quite taken aback. What? He didn't tell you? He concealed it from you? He informs her that I haven't been on the payroll for two months now. He doesn't enlighten her as to the reasons for my departure. My wife cries as she tells me what he said.

This announcement puts my mind at rest. Truth be told, I was planning to make a full disclosure, not for moral reasons, which are of little concern to me, but to explain the absence of income.

I reassure my wife: everything will turn out all right, honey. In no time. Real soon. Tomorrow. Don't worry. I'll do what-ever it takes to find a new job.

I make all kinds of crazy promises. Better days ahead, the moon, an electric dryer. I think I left something out: love. Let me start over. I make all kinds of crazy promises. Better days ahead, love, the moon, an electric dryer. The usual conjugal talk that I've finally adopted as my own, and which I produce as well as the next fellow. As proof, my wife dries her tears. She's renewed her hopes. Hope is a weed, Doctor. Try as we may to uproot it, it springs right back. We'll get by, I tell her. She falls asleep. She snores.

The next morning, my wife goes to the doctor's. Her stomach pains have flared up again. The doctor orders that she avoid any kind of vexation. She gets back around noon. I've prepared a meal, at great cost of time and effort, and set the table. We sit down to lunch. My wife then notices that the table still bears traces of breakfast. Coffee stains and bread-crumbs litter the oilcloth, which I didn't take the trouble to clean off. You didn't wipe the table, my wife exclaims. You set the table without cleaning it off first, she cries, as if I had committed some kind of crime. I don't respond. It's awful, she sobs. I don't understand what's so awful about it. My wife cries. I watch her cry. I've been less annoyed for some time now by my wife's tears. Something hard in me softens. My wife calms down. She dries her tears. She says: What's the matter with you, anyway? You're getting strange. I reply: I'm feeling exactly the reverse. I feel perfectly fine. I'm getting stronger. I feel an increasing sense of self-possession. Of obedience only to myself. What about the job? she says. I don't give a shit about the job, I tell her. I've banished work from my life, as one of its most tiresome formalities. (I could hardly state it more plainly.) At this, my wife starts sobbing again. This is becoming a habit.

The only question that interests me, I tell her, is this: how to gain a foothold in the void. How to achieve the composure that anchors you to the earth.

And once again, sobs.

—∞—

A month elapses. Or two. Or ten.

At regular intervals, and at my wife's behest, I go register at the unemployment office. So, here I am, finally affiliated with an organization, I who was so recalcitrant.

As it turns out, finding a job is the least of their concerns. Which is fine, since I burn with no great desire to work.

As the days go by, I feel gripped by an immense idleness. I stumble over my untied shoelaces, lacking the strength to bend over and tie them. Putting on and removing clothing have become tedious chores. If I weren't afraid of attracting my wife's attention, I would go to bed fully clothed.

I often wonder what they do all day, all those people who, like me, are wholly lacking any spirit of enterprise. I don't feel like doing anything. Nothing except walking and sleeping.

My wife says I've really hit rock bottom.

Yet I feel as if my feet were no longer touching the ground.

My wife says I'm a little crazy, that it's a bad seed, probably on my father's side. To revel in such a state of inertia, you have to be a little nuts, asserts my wife.

I think she is right. A bad seed has sprouted in me, taken me over. A seed of madness or of something else, I can't say just yet. The seed has now become a tree with branches coming out of my mouth. Perhaps, I muse, I might end up like my mother's brother, in a mental hospital where they tie the insane to their bedposts and administer electroshock therapy (250 francs net profit for the doctor per session, Monsieur Jean told me). Or like the bums who sleep in cardboard boxes under the Châtelet tunnel. Or maybe like a criminal, I muse, without believing it. For I've never envisioned crime, Doctor, outside the realm of the imaginary.

I have stopped going to the café des Platanes. Pinaud's conversations were starting to bore me toward the end. I'm tired of hearing about other people's misery. I wonder, by the way, Doctor, how you manage to put up with your line of work. Lord, how can you stand it, listening all day to people whining? It's downright unwholesome. And what do you do with all the misfortune people confide in you? Don't you ever feel like screaming and telling your patients to just shut up?

I continue my explorations of the countryside. But it's crucial that I not be spotted hanging around in the neighborhood, since the neighbors are not supposed to know that I've lost my job. In my wife's words, it's a dishonor that must be kept under wraps.

So, I start venturing further and further from the house.

When I get home, my wife greets me with a sour face. Did you find a job? This is clearly all she knows how to say. And if I try to make light of it, I have a knot in my stomach, she complains, kneading it with the palm of her hand.

Every evening, Doctor, my wife harasses me with questions about my job search, despite the advice of her mother, who urges her over the phone not to torment me. If you keep pestering him, he'll dump you, her mother drills into her, and if you end up by yourself, flat broke, growing old alone and flat broke, it's the worst thing in the world that could happen.

Every evening when I get home, my wife waves an unpaid bill in my face. One thousand six hundred francs for water, she grumbles, handing me the blue and white printout, as if I didn't know how to read. I take the form and shove it in my pocket. My pocket is full of unpaid bills.

I don't quite grasp, Doctor, why my wife is in such a bad mood. Especially since I give in to all her whims: I wipe my feet before coming into the house, I don't read in the garden anymore. In fact, I don't read at all.

I've even stopped grousing about doing chores. I finally understood that, in my wife's eyes, intentions are worth just as much as actions. Example: when it's time to clear the table, if I start by removing the glasses, my wife, encouraged by my good will, takes it upon herself to do the rest. That's how I proceed with all the other household chores. I hint at an action, my wife completes it.

I strive to maintain the habits I'd developed while I was still working. I get up at 8 o'clock and dress properly. My wife says we have to save face. Face? It's me I'm trying to save, for the love of Christ.

—∾—

I haven't been to the oak grove for a week now.

I'm not doing anything.

Good for nothing, gripes my wife.

Very good, I say.

That drives her crazy.

What a cross to bear, she sighs, kneading her stomach with both hands.

172

I suggest taking up knitting, like the *Solitaires* of Port-Royal. A little muffler, I tell her, a little cap for winter, or some nice mittens.

I return, I get mocked and bad-mouthed.

It would be untrue, however, to say that I do nothing. I excel at an exercise that requires great skill: ridding my cat of fleas. I proceed as follows: I keep a careful watch over the beast's belly to scout out the bugs; I then trap the flea, with stunning dexterity, between the thumb and index finger of my right hand; and with the sharp point of my left thumbnail, I slice the pest in two. I rarely miss. It's an achievement to be proud of.

Twenty-One

I HAVEN'T GOTTEN DRESSED IN A WEEK. I MEAN I SPEND THE day in my pajamas, an outfit which, if I'm to believe my wife's prickly quips, does little to enhance my sexual assets.

I don't leave my room anymore.

I've suspended time. Whether it be long or short, I don't care. I stay in bed, as motionless as a spider, and from inside my eyes I watch the wall slowly crack.

I've ceased my soliloquies. I'm no longer interested in myself.

Sometimes I wonder whether I'm not going to merge with the wall. And disappear. I touch my face to make sure I'm still alive. My face is warm, and it moves. But is that proof enough? My wife thinks I'm a lost soul. I, on the other hand, know that I have found myself again. Or rather, found for the first time, after long searches and delays. My wife comes knocking at the door at regular intervals. Open up, please, open the door. Sometimes she loses her temper. Open up, or I'll beat the door down, and she rushes at the door and pounds at it with her fists until they bruise. Open up, I'm telling you, or I'll call the police.

At regular intervals, my wife leaves a tray of food outside the door. I don't go get it until I know she's gone. From time to time, a noise will stir me from my reverie, if one can call reverie this slow sliding into the void.

Sometimes, my wife approaches the door and utters phrases whose meaning I don't quite grasp, but which sound threatening.

One morning, she announces that she's leaving for her parents'. I hear myself reply: Say hello to Mom for me. My reflexes are still good. I'm delighted.

I hear crying, doors slamming. Then silence.

Days pass, probably quite a few days.

One day, hunger forces me out of bed. I walk through all the rooms. My legs are wobbly. I go into the bathroom. I look at myself in the mirror. It sends back such a terrifying image that I almost react like my cat, which growls when it sees itself in a mirror, believing it's spied an enemy. Frankly, I look repulsive. I decide to wash and shave. I remove my pajamas, which give off a peculiar odor, and I take a shower.

Then, I go to the kitchen. I notice some coins on a side table. That gives me the idea that I could leave, but where to go? I climb up into the attic. In the dim light, I see a suitcase. I open it, put a copy of Pascal's *Pensées* inside. I add a pair of socks and a sweater. The suitcase doesn't fasten. I tie it closed with some string. I get dressed. I manage to tie my shoes. I comb my hair. I leave.

I walk for a long time. I cross through a small town. In a shop window, I see a help-wanted ad for clearing underbrush. Why not? I clear underbrush. For Monsieur and Madame Amiel, that's their name. They're nice to poor folks. You can tell. They even offer me coffee. Which they bring out to me in the garden. So that I don't get their house dirty. Good folks. I ask them whether they don't have any other chores for me. Laundry, ironing, I'm willing to do anything, I'm that hungry.

Very few people, it seems to me, know what real hunger is.

The Amiels don't have any other jobs for me. They apologize.

Then the idea occurs to me that I could press on, all the way to the capital, where I expect to derive great comfort at the sight of my fellow man.

I catch a bus for Paris. I get off at Place de la République. I walk along Boulevard Voltaire. I give a swift kick to a tin can, sending it rolling along the sidewalk. A few passersby glance at me warily. Is my outward appearance troubling? And what of the inward? Everyone else is walking by very quickly. City folks aren't as likeable as I had imagined, I think to myself. I'm going to have to be exceedingly cautious around them. Speak softly. Gesticulate less. Lower my eyelids (blessed barrier!).

I enter the first café I come across. I ask for the owner. I'm looking for work, sir. Anything will do. I've thought hard about it, but I can't think of a job that's any less degrading than another.

Less? asks the owner.

Less what? I say.

Never mind, says the owner. And he inspects me, head to toe.

I recall that the sole of my right shoe has come unglued in front. A detail that couldn't escape the owner's notice, I conclude, and I feel myself growing weak.

Married?

No.

Children?

No.

Do you know the prices?

No.

The owner suggests I try on the uniform left behind by the last waiter. The trouser legs stop short of my ankles. I look ridiculous. Parisian cafés are packed with loafers with nothing to do but take notice of trivial details, and I fear they'd laugh at me. On the contrary. No one pays me the slightest attention.

I begin my shift. It's not as hard as one would think. Most of the customers don't leave me any tips. Is it because of my uniform? Or is there something etched in my face, some ineffable quality that inspires contempt?

On break, the second waiter elaborates on his dreams: save as much money as he can to buy a restaurant in Montpellier where he'll be the undisputed boss. The idea makes him giddy. It makes him glow. That's not my notion of an ideal, I say. He nearly drops his tray. That's the first time anyone has been unenthusiastic about his plan.

We go back to our shift. The second waiter talks a lot to the customers, and everyone seems to appreciate his stupidity. An exalted, aggressive, rousing kind of stupidity. When he has a free moment, the second waiter asks me, sardonically, So what's your notion of an ideal? It's to gain a foothold in the void, I reply. This answer leaves him openmouthed. But he's quick to recover his poise. He puts the peculiar answer out of his mind. And to prove he's clever, he asks me: And this little scheme of yours, do you think it'll make money?

That evening, the owner informs me that my tryout has not been satisfactory. Ought we to conclude so hastily, I tell him, when all things lead us to the end? Am I not being judged a trifle too summarily? Is this not the foremost failing of our times? Why such a rush, Monsieur Café Owner, to rule me out? The café owner and the second waiter exchange amused glances. The eagle is so beautiful, I say to them, before it swoops down on its prey. The owner bursts out laughing. He pays me what he owes me. Together with a couple of tips, the whole affair amounts to some 200 francs. Enough to get by quite well for two or three days. I decide to stay in the city. This brief experiment has renewed my fondness for human contact.

I remember all of a sudden an acquaintance who lives nearby. A leather worker where my father had me do a stint as apprentice when I was fourteen. (Papa wanted me to learn a craft that paid better than his. Papa thought there was a future in the leather trade. And he placed great hopes in my social advancement.) I ring the leather worker's doorbell. He comes to the door. An odor of leather permeates the apartment. He doesn't recognize me. I introduce myself. He doesn't look overly enthusiastic. I give him a brief outline of my circumstances, and his enthusiasm drops another notch. His wife approaches. She's wearing a checkered apron. She mistakes me for a Jehovah's Witness, and she warns, while wiping her hands on her checkered apron, that their family doesn't get mixed up with religion. The leather worker appears terribly ill at ease, but then quickly recovers. Though he is overflowing with the milk of human kindness, he explains, the size of his present premises doesn't allow him to take in lodgers. There's something I admire. This spirit of decision-making, this way of taking charge. A man of great caliber, I think, bound for the grandest of destinies.

For a few moments, I contemplate moving in on them by force. I think, if I move in on them, the leather worker won't have the heart to turn me away. It often happens that people move in, overstaying their welcome, and it's practically impossible to dislodge them. This situation recurred a number of times at our home in the country, especially when we first moved out there. People from the city would arrive at our place on Saturday morning to breathe the fresh air, and wouldn't leave until Sunday evening, as if it were perfectly natural that we should have them stay over. And for two endless days, we had to make their beds, cook their meals, and what's worse, put up with their artsy conversations, their thoughtful countenance at the sight of cow dung, their plangent elegies in the presence of ineffable bucolic happiness. Not for a single moment did they ever wonder whether they were putting us out, whether their presence annoyed us, whether it was driving us crazy. They simply stuck around, and neither my wife nor I had the nerve to evict them. I had to make myself obnoxious and unpleasant before they finally realized they were the ones who were being horribly obnoxious and unpleasant.

In the present circumstance, I drop my plan. I take leave of the leather worker, good luck in the leather business, and I head for the Saint-Lazare station, the ideal spot, it seems, to make friends. I enter the main terminal. I make my way toward a group of winos who are acting strangely merry. The bottle, one of them murmurs as I approach. The bottle is instantly hidden away in a backpack.

I go sit on a bench, next to a woman. She's blond, she's ugly, she's pale and puffy, with a persistent odor emanating from her body. She turns toward me. In a wine-slurred voice, she asks me what I do for a living. The question is cosmic. I reply succinctly: I'm searching for how to gain a foothold in the void. This answer leaves her at a loss for words. She gazes at me in a daze, then falls into a deep slumber, stirred by grunts and horrible visions. I get up. I look for an available bench.

There's one next to the door that has remained vacant because of the draft. I stretch out on it, and I also fall asleep.

In the morning, I wake numb. I don't know which way to head. I wander where my humor leads me, or, as I should say, my ill-humor. People stare at me warily. Is it my wrinkled clothes? A look on my face?

I stroll down the most beautiful avenue in the world, and I see nothing but tasteless advertisements and the every-day crowds in their Sunday best. I walk up and down and all around the streets of the most beautiful city in the world, and I perceive nothing but roaring traffic, turmoil and foul smells. By evening, I arrive at Place de la Bastille, location of the most beautiful opera house in the world, and I stumble onto a glass-clad edifice, very ugly, very grey, soulless.

Perched atop his column, the *Génie de la Liberté,* with a star planted on its forehead, is poised to leap into the void.

I walk for part of the night. I sleep standing up. It's a position like any other, after all.

Dawn breaks. With my few remaining coins, I decide to sit down at a café. Perhaps I could freshen up a bit. At a nearby table sits a man armed with electronic devices. The new man, I say to myself, here is the new man. He's wearing a cell phone on his belt, like a gun. Suddenly, he draws the weapon, spits a few words into the device, then smugly tosses back his espresso in one gulp. This man accomplishes everything in a rush. Is he in such a hurry to advance toward death? He repeats the phone operation several more times. His correspondents, snatched from a sound sleep, must have a hard time carrying on a normal conversation. Once these tasks are performed, the new man athletically removes a laptop from his briefcase and taps away energetically, then tucks it back in place and dashes off down the street.

To my left, a young man stands, madly pressing the buttons of an electronic device composed of a screen where images appear and disappear at a dizzying rate, emitting strange sounds (the sound of a man drowning). The latest gear, I think, for gaining a foothold in the void, for anchoring oneself in the vastness of the world.

I open a newspaper left behind on the table near mine.

> Bloody chase in the Bois de Vincennes.
> Two young anarchists, aged 19 and 23
> open fire on police officers.
> The gun battle kills five: three police officers,
> a taxi driver and one of the gunmen.

The young men were armed with a .38 Special police weapon they had stolen from the police pound at Pantin. Here again, I said to myself, are instruments that I've yet to learn how to handle in order to gain a foothold in the void.

Above this article appears a headline: Lose weight by hypnosis. It doesn't hold my attention.

The idea pops into my mind to go rob the alms box in a church, something I'd read about in certain Spanish novels. I enter Notre Dame. The dim light is just what is needed. It seems designed especially for thieving. Catholics know how to do things right, I think to myself. I head toward an alms box, after making the sign of the cross to fool the afflicted kneeling in prayer. Imagine my surprise to find the box empty! Traditions are disappearing. What a shame!

What to do now?

Sell hot chestnuts? But how in the name of Jesus do you get the fruit in the first place?

Dress up like Santa Claus? What season is it now? Winter, I suppose. Given the cold.

Cry out, Help! Help! right there in the street, at the top of my lungs, so that someone will finally look me in the eye?

But I need only observe the closed faces of my fellow men scurrying off, some to their trough, some to their kennel, to conclude that the plan is hopeless, even perilous.

Do some acrobatic act, then pass the hat among the crowd of onlookers? But what was I thinking? I don't have a hat anymore.

Night falls. I'm weary. On the side of a police van parked at Place de la Nation, I read: Help for the homeless. The shelter they have in mind hardly seems hospitable. I'd rather sleep in a doorway.

I keep moving on. I walk a few meters more. Then I slip down onto the sidewalk, exhausted, and fall asleep.

I wake with a start. I hear the noise of footsteps all around me. I open my eyes. I see nothing but feet. I must be dreaming, I think. Men in uniform lift me up and load me into their van. I'm not dreaming anymore. They hand me a chocolate bar. I accept it. I'm too weary to protest.

We drive along a highway. The van stops in front of the hospice, the Maison de Nanterre. I enter. It's hell. There's nothing more to be said.

I manage to escape in the night.

I forget my suitcase.

Here I am, relieved of anything superfluous.

But am I still human?

I walk for a long while.

I leave the city.

Since I don't know where I'm going, since I'm hungry, since I'm thirsty, since the garbage cans I come across are all empty, since I'm out of money, since I'm filthy, unkempt and poorly clothed, I decide to go to my father's. What happens next, Doctor, you already know.

SELECTED DALKEY ARCHIVE PAPERBACKS

FOR A FULL LIST OF PUBLICATIONS, VISIT:
www.dalkeyarchive.com

SELECTED DALKEY ARCHIVE PAPERBACKS

FOR A FULL LIST OF PUBLICATIONS, VISIT:
w w w . d a l k e y a r c h i v e . c o m